Magiks
and the
Tale of Two Kings

Loup Gajigianis

the Enchanted Chronicle

The Enchanted Chronicle

The Enchanted Chronicle Series
Text copyright © 2024 by Janet Loup Maupin Gajigianis
Published by Enchanted Chronicle LLC
Illustrations by Arthur Bowling III
Cover by Miblart

All rights reserved. No part of this publication may be duplicated, manufactured, distributed, transmitted, used, or reproduced in any manner whatsoever, including but not limited to information storage, photocopying, recording, or other electronic or mechanical methods without the prior written permission of the publisher, except for the use of brief quotations in critical articles and reviews permitted by copyright law. Inquiries for permission requests outside of those terms should be addressed to the publisher and consent must be in writing.
All rights reserved

The only person I can dedicate this story to is my dad; A brilliant man, who regales me with stories of cultures, histories, invasions, and wars—whether I want to hear them or not.

Usually, I do.

It's a man's own mind, not his enemy or foe,
that lures him to evil ~ Gautama Buddha

CONTENTS

PROLOGUE

CHAPTER ONE
THE RETURN OF THE PRINCE

CHAPTER TWO
THE WARRIOR'S WISDOM

CHAPTER THREE
THE WARLOCK'S GUILE

CHAPTER FOUR
THE JINN'S WAY

CHAPTER FIVE
THE SHADOW'S CHOICE

CHAPTER SIX
THE KING'S FALLACY

AUTHOR BIO

AFTERWARD

Prologue

One warlock, one warrior, and two kings. The story that changed the magik world.

Nearly one and a half thousand years ago, in a wondrous place where wizards and fairies were plenty and sorcery wasn't just a tale told to children, many great kingdoms were governed by magiks. In the region of the Islamic empire, before the reign of the Abbasids in Bagdad, two magical kingdoms, hidden from humans, were ruled by the most powerful brothers across the lands; Mighty kings who believed the power of shapeshifters and shadow walkers was untapped.

MAGIKS AND THE TALE OF TWO KINGS

As princes, during the age when shapeshifters and shadow walkers were known only as changers, and their magic was feeble, the brothers were inseparable. They played together, grew together, laughed together, and side-by-side toyed with the limitations of their power. Prince Kazar believed in the way of shapeshifting. He turned himself into objects and even embodied citizens of his kingdom. However, by taking the full forms of others, he was also bound by their weaknesses. As a table, he could not breathe, and as an old man, his limbs were weak, and his body ached.

His brother, Prince Zaeg, didn't like accepting the weaknesses of other bodies and forms. Thus, he discovered the magic of shadowshifting. He turned into shadows, dark as the evening gloom, and stalked the palace. He practiced routinely, until he was a fearsome changer, and enjoyed pranking the palace guards with his unfathomable power. The two brothers loved each other dearly and were rarely seen apart. But, alas, as kings, a rift formed between them, for each believed they had discovered the best way to conquer the magical limitations of changers.

After the death of their father, the two brothers split his kingdom into two great empires; The Kingdom of Shadow Walkers took the lands south of the Euphrates River and east of the Nile. The Kingdom of Shapeshifters took the northern lands, from the Black Sea to the Indus River. For decades, each king devoted his life to expanding the magical limitations of changers. Their knowledge spread like wildfire beyond the borders of their lands and across the world.

Chapter One

The Return of the Prince

King Kazar

The distant horizon pinkened. A soft spread of orange cascaded across the hills, reflecting a golden hue off the grassy tips. A subtle glow illuminated the high, domed chamber where King Kazar sat impatiently. It was the same vaulted solar that once belonged to his father, the King of Kings, and it had changed little through the years. Now it was his chamber, though he rarely used it except for special occasions like this. His tired face turned to the windows as the sun rose. *Finally,* he thought. A king was not made to wait for anyone, not even the sun. Dawn should have risen hours ago. For if the king had to wake, so should the sky, and the birds, and then the people to follow. Instead, he'd woken alone, save for the servants tasked with gowning him. But if he had magic like Azhir, the stubborn warlock residing in his palace, he would have forced the moon from the horizon and commanded dawn sooner. For by the afternoon sun, his brother would march across his borders, and the fate of their kingdoms would be decided.

Even now, a servant fumbled oafishly over his embroidered silk robes. They were black as wet ink. The color matched his dark hair and ebony eyes as he narrowed them. With his life spent as a royal, he had acquired a regal demeanor, but black added the daunting edge that suited him well. The servant continued to fumble, and the king grumbled quietly. A deft pair of hands pulled the servant away and skillfully finished the task.

The heavy tap of a heeled boot announced the arrival of one of his men-at-arms. King Kazar didn't bother to look up. Only Firoza, the fiercest fighter in his kingdom and captain of his guard, would dare enter without announcing herself first.

"Has General Harun arrived?" He asked without turning. He let the servant finish. There was no reason to move yet. If only the man would hurry.

"Yes, My King," Firoza replied. "Moments ago. Along with five thousand soldiers. He is hiding them around the palace and in the city as you commanded."

"And the Elves?" His voice curled. The daunting edge in his tone drove the servant back or perhaps the man was finally finished, but he didn't bother to check. King Kazar turned and faced his warrior captain. Gold earrings dazzled her sharp features, and dark hair tumbled down her back. Two glittering wings fluttered behind her. If he hadn't known she was more dangerous than all of his soldiers, he would have been captivated by her beauty. Deadly knives decorated her hair, her earrings picked locks, and her wristlets were armor.

"They have refused the invitation as you predicted."

"Good. We don't need their interference." King Kazar grunted. "Leave us," he ordered the servants, and they departed directly. When they were alone, he spoke softer and with an openness that he shared with few, though it was several moments before the words came. "My brother has always been an ambitious prince, and now, as ruler of half my father's kingdom, he has pushed magic beyond what I ever thought possible." The king stared down at his marred hands. Years of breaking the boundaries of magic had left deep scars that even the innate power of changers couldn't heal. Nor the Elven elixirs made of ash from The Land of Fire. "His army has tripled the size of mine, and with it he has taken other lands. Azhir warns me against an alliance." By habit, he put on the gloves he had accustomed himself to wearing. The soft leather creased familiarly over his marred hands. "They say my brother can soar weightlessly across the lands for as many miles as he chooses." His voice tightened. It ached with regret and sorrow.

"We have been experimenting too."

"Yes. But with shadowshifting, my spies say there are no limits to the possibilities."

"There are limits to all things, My King."

"Yet, I hear of none."

"Just because you do not hear it nor see it doesn't mean it is not true." Firoza hesitated before suggesting, "Ask your brother to confide in you and share the challenges of the shadow ways."

"How—when my brother and I do not even speak? He is my blood, and I barely know him. Once, when we were children, nothing could have torn us apart. But now, our kingdoms are split with walls, our palaces are filled with spies, and I must hide that I am in trouble."

"Perhaps this secrecy is not necessary. Tell your brother of the troll raids. Tell him of the impending invasion. Tell him tonight, at the celebration."

King Kazar faltered. He stared back at Firoza, wanting it to be so easy. But years of bearing the weight of a king had hardened him. "I cannot. Not until I am sure he can be trusted. The safety of my kingdom rests on my shoulders." A firm line set in his lips. He crossed the chamber and unfolded a map across a weathered table. His gloved finger traced the marked points along the boundaries of his empire and the lands beyond. "Look here. Everyone is a danger to our kingdom. We are surrounded. The mountain trolls have come down from the Alps and crossed the Danube River. Sea trolls attacked our southern ports by the Arabian Sea. Desert trolls have gathered on our eastern borders along the Khyber Pass. The elves wait for our army to deplete. The fairies do nothing. Threats gather on all sides. And then finally to the South is my brother, who wishes that every changer had learned the way of shadowshifting instead of shapeshifting." He rolled up the map and tucked it away. His saddened gaze locked on the captain of his guard. "We must only let him see a strong, unbreakable empire of shapeshifters. One whose alliance he will wish to join."

"But if you were—"

"I must be certain you understand this." His eyes hardened to a withering glare that narrowed, as was a king's habit when being firm. "Or perhaps you aren't fit to be head of my guard."

Firoza bowed deeply. "I seek only to be the blade that protects you, and the voice that guides you." Her voice didn't tremble. As always, it was genuine and strong.

King Kazar's hardness faded, and he sighed. Bearing the weight of a king was wearisome, and he wished he could be a boy again, playing in the fields with his brother.

"Rise," he commanded, ashamed of his quick anger. Firoza was his most trusted soldier. She had followed him to every battle and fought beside him, guarding him with her life. Over the years, she had become family. And though she wasn't an advisor, her words held weight. He wished to ask for forgiveness, but Kings did not ask for such things. His voice softened. "My apologies, Old Friend."

"None is needed from a great king." Firoza reminded him. He smiled lightly. In many ways, they thought alike. It came from the many years they had walked these palace halls together. He had known her since days of her exile and the anguish she suffered from losing her own kind in order to save them from war with his own kingdom, and she had known him from the happiest days, when his children were born, and the heartbroken ones when his wife had died. "Tell me your plan," she said assuredly.

King Kazar rubbed the bridge of his nose, tiredly. "My father would have wanted peace. He would have wanted our kingdoms to remain one empire. We were wrong to divide it." He moved to the window and stared out as far as he could see. "Even now, troll armies assemble beyond our borders. They envy our lands. Our prosperity. Our wealth. They want our trade routes and our fertile land. They may even have the strength to take it. If they attack, they'll kill everyone. And those that live will have to flee."

"You've built a great army, My King. You could defend us."

"That may be true. But many lives would be lost. "I need my brother's help. I must convince him to join me." He turned his back to the window. Convincing his brother to unite would not be easy. "I want this to be the grandest celebration in magic history! But my brother must be kept safe. Our enemies will not want us to make an alliance. And if the trolls see him approaching, they may attack."

"He will be in danger," she agreed. "Should we warn him of the danger beyond the trade routes?"

"No. Not until I'm ready. I want to tell him of the coming days myself. Fortify the roads and send soldiers to escort him to the city. While he is here, you will guard him personally."

"As you command." Firoza bowed deeply, her armored hair swung forward, revealing daggers down her back. She had never failed him, and for that, she had risen higher than any exiled soldier should have been allowed, even if she was a fairy. She would not fail him. Not when peace for the entire realm was at stake.

By mid-morning, the palace was buzzed with life. Servants bustled from chamber to chamber carrying flour for cakes, sweeping mud from the stone hearth, and preparing for the elaborate celebration. By noon, the cavalcade arrived. Nearly a hundred of the shadow kingdom's finest soldiers, richest merchants, cleverest advisers, and noblest magiks marched past the palace gardens. King Kazar spotted his brother amongst them easily. He rode the back of a manticore, surrounded by beautiful dancers that turned into shadows and back again, in rhythm with the music.

The procession drove his subjects wild. They cheered and threw favors, celebrating the return of their lost prince, now King of the Shadow Lands. King Kazar watched his brother laugh handsomely at their adoration, with the natural charm he had as a child, though he was a man now. Dark hair hung over his brow. His face had hardened and matured, and his beard had filled in, angling out from his chin. His face was nearly unrecognizable except for the mischievous play in his smile and the way he dazzled the crowd.

"They adore him," King Kazar admitted reluctantly. He tried to remember if their faces lit up for him in the same way.

"He is your father's heir," Firoza said shrewdly. "As are you."

"And yet they love him more." He had no trouble remembering the many times his brother had won the affections of those around them. "Look at my kingdom. They have forgotten he was the cause of the divided empire, and that he abandoned all those who did not follow in his ways."

Firoza chose her words carefully. "You are a forbidding king," she admitted truthfully. "He is playful, and his charisma is easy to love."

"He is a better king then."

"The art of enchanting others does not equal that of moral character." Firoza's voice stiffened surely. "You've rebuilt treaties with your neighbors, expanded the lands of your kingdom, spread the knowledge of shapeshifting, and brought wealth and peace to all. Look again. They have prospered because of you."

King Kazar turned back to the parade. A ruckus broke out below, and he watched his brother show off amidst the swooning crowd. The quarrel quelled, and there was no denying that his brother had always stolen the hearts of those around him. Lost in the enchantment, King Kazar leaned further over the balustrade and longed to be beside his brother, dazzling the crowd.

By chance, King Zaeg's glance flickered up and caught sight of King Kazar. His impish smile vanished. Hurt, hardened over time, flickered across his features, and he gazed away. At the base of the palace, he dismounted and strode up the grand staircase to greet his brother for the first time in years.

King Kazar returned inside the high-vaulted solar and braced himself. Cool bumps tingled down his arms and he shivered. Strangely, he could not remember the last time he had been nervous. He watched the closed chamber door. The safety of his kingdom depended on making peace with his brother, this King of the Shadow Lands, now a stranger to him. And if he did not make an alliance, his kingdom would be torn apart before the next summer's end. Of that, he was certain.

King Zaeg strode through the doors, pausing only when he caught sight of King Kazar. His back stiffened. But to conceal his hesitation, he smiled handsomely and swaggered forward to greet the King of the Shapeshifters.

King Kazar clasped his brother in a tight embrace. "Welcome, Brother," he grunted uncomfortably. Forgiveness was hard for men, harder for brothers, but hardest for kings. "It's been too long." A feeling of longing squeezed his chest, and he hugged his brother tighter.

King Zaeg blushed at the embrace. When they broke apart, the warm flush lingered, and he circled the vaulted chamber that had once been their father's, his cheerful spirit returning. "Thirty years," he counted.

"Thirty-three." King Kazar corrected and cut off abruptly at the awkwardness that followed. He inspected his brother closely. Dark shadows swelled beneath his eyes, and there was a thinness about his handsome features—tolls from his own pursuit of magic. Memories flooded back from untroubled times. "The last time I saw you in this room, you chased the tutor from the solar." King Kazar's eyes glinted humorously. "You demanded he not to tell you what was impossible. That nothing was impossible. He only lacked imagination."

King Zaeg smiled crookedly. "You remember that?"

King Kazar smiled bigger. It felt foreign and stiff but good. "I'll never forget it."

King Zaeg's face lightened before his brow tightened, and his smile dimmed. He walked to the window where their mother used to sit, clearly lost in memories. "Why have you called me here?"

King Kazar's chest squeezed. There was a time when his brother would have come to him gladly, without suspicions or doubts. Now they were older and wiser, from ruling their kingdoms. His brother was too keen to be fooled for long. But when the words of the troll raids came, King Kazar could not speak them. "We must reconcile. We must align our kingdoms, join our armies, reinforce our borders, and encourage our subjects to live together as friends."

"Align? That may not be possible. Too many years have passed."

"It is my wish."

King Zaeg swallowed hard. "Your wish?"

"Yes. I would like to re-unite with my brother and for our kingdoms to become allies again."

"I'll admit I'm surprised." He lifted his eyes and met his brother's gaze. "We have spent many years at odds. Shapeshifters and shadow walkers have come to distrust each other. Fear each other even."

"Which was never our intent." King Kazar's eyes cut into his brother's, meaning the words fully. "We meant only to pursue our own ways of magic."

"In that, I agree." King Zaeg's taut muscles loosened, and he slouched against the window. "When we began our dreams of evolving our power, it never occurred to me that I would lose my brother. Perhaps, it was best you sent for me."

King Kazar let out a breath that he didn't realize he was holding onto. "I worried you would refuse my invitation."

"I thought of it," admitted King Zaeg.

"But you didn't?"

"We're brothers." King Zaeg straightened from the window. His carefree smile returned, and the handsome sparkle played in his eyes. "Why should I not come, when my brother asks for me?"

A wistful smile wavered over King Kazar's features. "Because I pursued a different path than you. One that you did not favor."

"It was not your choice of path that drove me away. It was your disapproval of mine," King Zaeg pointed out to him. "I wished to rule our father's realm together. I never wanted a kingdom separate from yours."

"Forgive me then," King Kazar's voice choked. "I feared your abandonment of the ancient rules of magic. I see I was wrong. Let us start anew. We will learn from each other. Grow from our newfound knowledge. And turn our kingdoms into brothers like they once were."

King Zaeg's voice wavered slightly, "Do you mean it, Brother?"

"I do." King Kazar pulled his brother into a tight embrace, meaning it truly in the depths of his heart. "I have missed you."

Mist dappled in King Zaeg's eyes, and they stood like that for several moments.

Feeling whole again, King Kazar released him. "I have a gift for you—crafted by Azhir Izzat Ibn Al-Ghaazi himself."

King Zaeg's surprise curled into a grin. "The rumors are true then? Azhir is here? The Great Warlock of the East?"

"In the caverns beneath this very palace, tinkering away."

"I must drop in and see what mischief I can find."

"Ha! You haven't changed a bit," laughed King Kazar. "But you must be tired from your journey. Use my solar as your own. Your guard may rest in the adjoining chambers while my captain, Firoza, and her strongest warriors watch over you." He gestured towards the adjoining door, and King Zaeg's guard eagerly followed it. "Rest. Tonight will be a glorious celebration."

King Kazar left, feeling lighter than he had in years. Outside, he spoke to Firoza. "He wishes to align our kingdoms as much as I!" His voice burst from his chest, and he rocked forward in his regal slippers like a child, but Firoza showed no change in manner, and she replied with a straight face.

"Is he not a threat to your border, as you said?"

"I was mistaken."

"Yet, you did not tell him of the troll raids."

"When the time is right—I will do it then." Firoza's distrust was apparent, so King Kazar continued. "I believe him to be earnest. This may work as planned—No, better than planned. He misses me. I can tell."

Firoza toyed with the hilt of her dagger, as she did when considering matters of state. "It would appear so."

"I see your hesitation. Speak openly," the king urged. "Dare I hope that my kingdom is saved? Dare I dream to have my brother by my side once again?"

"You must always hope and dream, but you cannot take a few, carefully chosen words and form judgment of one's character," she said wisely.

"He is my brother."

"And a stranger. With no allegiance to you." She pointed to his chest where the map was hidden. "Not moments ago, you showed me that we truly are surrounded on all sides by those who wish to see us fall. You said no one could be trusted, not even King Zaeg."

King Kazar shook his head stubbornly. "We are brothers, and I was wrong. He is not as different as I thought. Nor has he changed much from when we were children."

"But this is your kingdom at stake," Firoza pressed. "Our lives depend on you."

King Kazar considered her, and his elation faded. His duties as king weighed down on his shoulders once more. "Thank you, Firoza. I don't know what I would do without your friendship. You are right of course. I cannot become blind for love of my estranged brother." He clasped his gloved hand on her armor. The black in his eyes sparkled as the threat of war prevailed in his thoughts once again. "Watch him carefully but keep him safe. My brother has reached the palace safely, but that does not mean he is no longer in danger. Our enemies know that if we align, our forces will be unstoppable. And when the trolls meet us in battle, the fairy king will no longer be able to sit idly by as they take the free lands. He will have to join us . . . or the trolls."

"He will not join the trolls," Firoza assured him, and as she once lived in the royal castle as a high-ranking officer, he believed her.

"I'm counting on it. I await the day he comes with gifts and apologies and beseeches to join my armies." He offered a coy smile. "I should make him beg."

"You are too great a king," Firoza reminded him.

"Then I shall enjoy the thought of it," he groused. With that, King Kazar shapeshifted. Feathers sprouted from his chest and back, his nose hardened, and he shrunk until he could stand in the palm of a warrior. Craving the wind and freedom of the skies, he took flight and soared through the palace window, feeling at ease for the first time in a long time. For his brother had returned, and once their kingdoms were united, the Fairy Kingdom would join his army, and his kingdom would be saved.

Perhaps, all would be well after all, he told himself.

Chapter Two
The Warrior's Wisdom

King Zaeg

The smell of freshly baked bread wafted in through the open windows as King Zaeg strolled through the elegantly furnished room. He knew his brother was outside the door. King Kazar was likely directing the staff or perhaps speaking with the beautiful warrior that guarded him. But he was certain his brother was still there, as he did not hear his footsteps fade down the hall. Though he was curious why his brother lingered, it did not bother him that he did so.

His brother honored him by giving up his own solar—the solar of their father, the King of Changers. And it was a welcome relief to give his personal guard the opportunity to rest. It had been a long, wearisome journey. One he never planned to take. But when he received word that his brother had called for him, he had gathered his council and left before the next full moon. A brother is a brother after all.

King Zaeg leaned over the balustrade. Below, dozens of carpenters, smiths, and merchants prepared for the celebration. They laughed and sang as they worked. His brother's kingdom had prospered far beyond anything he'd imagined. His own kingdom was poor compared to this spectacle below. He did not have the lavish imports, spices, nor colorful fabrics. He had none of this, but he had something else. His army was the greatest in the world. No company, command, nor artillery could face the Dark Shadow Walker Army without annihilation, and that was something to be proud of. His soldiers, both men and women, were the most skilled fighters across the world. His strength had kept the innocents of his kingdom safe. Still, the disparity of wealth disheartened him, and he wondered what choices, as king, his brother had made that were better than his own.

His brother had done well since they last met. It had been years since he stood in his parent's palace. While it looked the same it was so much brighter. In the halls, linen draperies had been replaced with reversible Damask. Cotton throws on the daybeds were swapped for silk and velvet. The divan beside him was covered in a rich brocade. He brushed his finger along the gold thread. Could their kingdoms truly be allies? If they were allies, would the Shadow Lands prosper like the Kingdom of Shapeshifters?

The voices outside his doorway quieted, and the sound of soldier's footsteps clambered down the hall. *Did my brother truly miss me?* he wondered. When they were children, Kazar had been his protector. They went everywhere together. *Surely now, my brother would do the same,* he told himself.

King Zaeg leaned over the balustrade deep in thought for some time as he watched the villagers below. A lone soldier quickened across the yard, and King Zaeg let his keen eyes trail after him. The sun gleamed off freshly polished armor. A curved sword glinted in the light, and a short dagger hung from the warrior's belt. The soldier glanced around uneasily. Then he scurried beneath the low-hanging rooftops. Using the roof as cover, he ducked out of sight.

King Zaeg's soft smile disappeared. His suspicious nature flooded with new thoughts. *Why was a soldier hiding inside of the palace gates? Who was he hiding from, and where was he headed? Why was he dressed for war, rather than the usual formal brocade soldiers wore at court?*

King Zaeg turned to the door where Firoza stood guard and listened. There was only silence. He strode into the middle of the solar. "Firoza?" He called, not certain she would answer, but then the door opened, and the beautiful warrior stepped inside.

"Ah. I wasn't sure you were still there. It was so quiet."

"So that the king's brother may rest," she replied.

"I see. Well, my personal guard will protect my chamber—if there happens to be a need. You're free to go. I'm sure my brother has need of you."

"My orders are to take watch outside your chamber. I'm to protect you while your guard recovers from the long journey."

King Zaeg forced back a frown of disappointment. He wasn't used to his orders being disregarded. Not even in the formal way this warrior did it. He kept his expression light. "If you wish to attend other matters, he will not hear of it from me." He offered a crooked smile that usually gave way to the effect he desired. It was a trick he learned young and mastered well.

"I have no other matters than to guard the King of the Shadow Lands. It is my honor to keep you safe." Firoza bowed.

"Hmm," he mumbled.

"What troubles you, King Zaeg?"

"My brother has not bothered to protect me for many years."

His gaze never left hers. He was known to be perceptive back home, but this warrior would not know he was skilled in reading emotions and deciphering intentions. "What has changed in my brother now?"

"My King wishes to strengthen the kingdoms and reunite with his brother," Firoza replied.

King Zaeg searched for signs in her features that she may be hiding a thought. When the moment passed and he didn't perceive any, he let his smile slip away. He waited for her to react to his silent change in disposition, that she might assume it meant more than it did. He watched for hesitancy in her features, or a wavering in her continuance that she may break if pressed.

There was none. He made a show of sighing. "As you wish then. I'll take a nap. Do not disturb me."

Firoza turned on her heel and moved lithely. Had he not seen it, he would not have known she moved at all. She paused by the door. "King Zaeg—"

"Yes?" His brow quirked, naturally curious, but beneath his serene mask, his pulse raced, and his heart pounded against his chest. Something was amiss. He could feel it.

"You should trust your brother. He is a good king."

King Zaeg's lips curled into his most handsome smile. "You are as loyal as stories have told."

"Fairies regard loyalty as the highest virtue. We are always loyal to our Kingdom," her voice trailed off, "if not our king."

King Zaeg caught the alter in her tone. He met her deep brown gaze. "So why is a fairy here in the Kingdom of Shapeshifters?"

Firoza answered without emotion like she had recited her story a hundred times. "I was an infantry soldier in the fairy army. I fought on the ground, sometimes in the frontline. Because of my skill, I was recruited to join a small, lethal unit that engaged in tactical operations. That entitled me to access to secret meetings and war plannings but also allowed me freedom to traverse the villages in search of spies.

At that time, tensions were brewing between our fairy king and the king of the shapeshifters. It was tension caused by my king and begun as a trifle that could have been resolved. My king was too proud. Tensions grew, and my kingdom prepared for war. We were evenly matched against the skin changers, and if we went to war, many innocent lives would be lost. The fairy kingdom was full of fear and sadness everywhere I traveled and when I attended the last meeting I realized my king did not care. I forged a letter to King Kazar requesting peace. I said the words my king should have voiced. I brokered the union that now stands. When it was discovered what I had done, I was found treasonous. King Kazar saved me. In exchange for my life, he traded one thousand of his finest swords, two herds of lamb, one year's worth of grain, and priceless goblin treasures. It was too much. But King Kazar said *peace for our kingdoms is worth more*. Those were the words my king should have said."

"That sounds like my brother."

"He offered me a position in his palace as a royal guard and a new home."

"And you rose to the rank you bear now," King Zaeg noted, impressed.

"Since then, the fairy king has calmed, and he offered great wealth for my return, with the promise I will be honored and given a title. Instead of accepting or refusing, King Kazar gave the choice to me. He gave me freedom in that gesture. I chose to stay here and serve as his captain. He is a good king," Firoza repeated.

"I think you are a good warrior and captain," he said honestly, surprising even himself. "I would have been honored if you had joined my guard. But my brother has always been the lucky one, and he found you instead."

Firoza bowed deeply. "It would have been my honor, King Zaeg."

A genuine smile stretched across his lips. *I like this warrior. I have not known her long, but she has courage and integrity that is rare to find.* His smile curled to the side in his playful way. *I bet she is talented with those weapons hiding in her hair. I see more in her boots, and I suspect her bosom too.* He shook his head and reminded himself of the sneaking soldier crossing yard below. *Something doesn't feel right.* He smiled out of politeness now, no longer interested in prolonging their conversation. "You may go."

Firoza bowed and left. The moment the door clicked shut behind her, King Zaeg's smile dissolved. Despite Firoza's gallant story, he knew a soldier readied for battle better than most. He glared at the door. He also knew when his chamber was being watched rather than guarded.

He pinched his chin between his fingers, and his thoughts raced. A moment later he crossed the room. He trod heavily, forcing the heel of his shoes to clap against the stone, and stopped in front of the bed. Instead of settling in for a nap, he shadowshifted. His majestic turban and robes whirled into soft wisps of black night. His skin flaked from his body, and he became a remnant of what he once was. *I will uncover the truth of the covert soldier for myself,* he decided. Soundlessly, he floated across the room, dove from the window, and soared across the yard.

The soft wind smelled of blossoms, cedar, and freshly baked bread. It was a welcome change to the stiffness of the chamber. The clear sky and cheerful magiks below settled him more than Firoza's reassuring words. There was no unease in the citizens of the kingdom.

It was hard to stay hidden in the daylight, but shapeshifters weren't accustomed to the magic of a shadowshifter. So the villagers excused his apparition as a this or that and went on about their business with hardly another thought. For that, the king of shadow walkers was able to move freely.

Weightlessly, he skimmed over the rooftops. As he traveled further from the palace, towards the edge of the kingdom, the streets emptied. Dry linen hung from lines, swaying in the breeze. Goats roamed the dirt roads freely.

LOUP GAJIGIANIS

Freshly cut wood waited to be burned. And tasks were left unfinished. It appeared the occupants had left suddenly and not returned. The homes were unlit and abandoned, and the sight did not alleviate the fear and hurt growing inside him.

He soon spotted the lone guard and followed him outside the gate, through a low mountain pass, and to a vast garrison. Tents, stables, and armories extended from the edge of the northern walls, beyond the trade routes, and to the foot of the nearest hilltop. Along the borders, armed soldiers stood in battle formation, alert and ready. More stood in watchtowers and turrets. Outside makeshift barracks, soldiers parried on a training ground, and cooks handed out the fatty portions of lamb and soup. Tacticians, counselors, and commanders scuttled in and out of a grand tent draped in the royal colors of his brother's kingdom.

What was left of King Zaeg's happiness vanished. His brother was preparing for war. But with whom? He frowned deeply. He had heard of no troubles with the Kingdom of Shapeshifters. The only kingdom at odds with the land of shapeshifters was his own. Sadness sunk in his chest, and his eyes burned. Could it be with him that his brother wished to make war? Could that be why he was invited to the city? His stomach twisted. *If it is true, it could only mean this celebration is a trap.* The churn in his stomach tightened and ached, making him sick.

As the realization settled in, a dark, furious haze crossed King Zaeg's shadowy face. Anger and hurt swelled, and his shadow whipped daringly. *My own brother prepares to make war against me.* His mind raced. *If I get a better look,* he calmed himself, *I can uncover what my brother truly intends, and if it really is to betray me. If I am clever enough, I can prepare my kingdom for this snare he has set.*

He could not force back the sick feeling as he soared higher, further than ever before, where the air was thin and cold. He stopped at a vantage point where he looked down over the edge of the kingdom. He spotted the lone guard that had led him to the garrison once again and dropped back at an alarming speed. He swooped and landed on the rooftop of a hastily built armory. A commanding soldier snarled and grabbed the soldier by his armor. "We're supposed to stay hidden! You can't go in and out of the city to see your if your woman is having an affair." Spit sprayed across the dirt.

"S-sorry, Sir."

"Sorry won't give back our position if we're exposed!"

"N-no one saw me, Sir!"

"How would you know if no one saw you?" he mocked.

"I-I," he fumbled.

The commander yanked him by the collar tighter, so that they were nose to nose. "If this visit with the shadow kingdom doesn't go exactly as the king planned, we will lose everything!"

"It won't happen again, Sir," the guard fumbled. A string of apologies and excuses followed, but the commanding soldier turned and stomped off.

From the rooftop, King Zaeg stared down in stupefied horror. Here it was—proof. His brother had assembled a grand army. There could only be one purpose—to take the Shadow Lands. Hurt bloated in his gut, and he did little to hide his shadow. Voices rose below. Soldiers pointed at his ghastly shade. Still, he didn't care. His brother had lied to him.

King Zaeg plunged from the rooftop. His shadow billowed out as he soared up and across the kingdom. Back at the palace, he swept through the crannies of the stone walls and landed in the chamber, leaving not a trace that he had ever left.

He felt numb. Sadness, hurt, and confusion made his thoughts blur. Too furious to be still, he stomped out onto the balcony and paced. He shot his furious gaze down on the villagers below. His brother had never approved of the way he'd forsaken the ancient rules of magic. He had called it unprincipled, dark, and corrupt. But just because something was unfamiliar didn't mean it was evil. King Zaeg trembled with fury. He never should have come back. He wiped a tear before it fell. What he needed was a plan. And the answer came, as his treacherous brother slipped across the courtyard below.

Chapter Three
The Warlock's Guile

King Kazar

King Kazar hurried across the palace grounds to visit the warlock as Azhir insisted on being regarded—rather than a wizard. All warlocks were wizards just more talented, and with some esteemed achievement that King Kazar didn't trouble himself to remember. And this eccentric warlock kept a workshop deep beneath the palace in an underground cavern. Why? King Kazar couldn't fathom. It was dark and damp. Torches never stayed lit, and boewood died in their lanterns.

Only fairy fire survived the thin, stale air, and it cast a golden hue that was frightening against the cavernous walls. Light was not much easier in the warlock's laboratory. Piles of books and vials collected dust from the stone ceiling. But still, Azhir had insisted. Here, his potions and brews stayed cool. And when King Kazar, desperate to avoid the deep labyrinth, tried to gift the warlock with the beautiful dome spire in place of the chilly cell, the warlock replied by taking both. Now the highest tower and the deepest dungeon belonged to an obstinate magic maker who hardly ever did as he was bade.

King Kazar took a last breath of fresh air and entered the stone cave. The cheerful festivities and lively music quickly became a faded dream as he trudged down the steps. The walls creaked and groaned at the intruder as if enchanted by magic, which it surely was, and the warlock's rats spoke. Their chitters echoed off the stones so it was impossible to tell if there were three or a hundred little vermin creeping inside the walls. King Kazar picked up his pace.

Inside the storeroom, potions brewed and bubbled. Usually, at least one book read itself aloud to the perked ears of the great warlock. Sometimes two books babbled together, competing for the attention of the bizarre magic maker. But today, they were silent and still, lying listlessly in their disorganized fashion. And inside the dungeon, the rats didn't speak. The only sound came from the soft crackle of the fireplace, for Azhir needed silence to complete a complicated piece of magic.

King Kazar hesitated at the entrance to the workshop, inside of which, Azhir leaned over his grimoire with a candle of golden fire. His long brown hair was braided out of his face, and his piercing black eyes devoured the words on the page. Flowing robes with sleeves trimmed at the elbows were belted at his waist with a round stone that changed colors with the skies. His pointed slippers stuck out beneath his robes, and they were oddly adorned with metal knickknacks like pliers, rods, picks, and spoons. He wasn't an old wizard, merely a century or so, but he was an unusual one. Yes, definitely unusual. And powerful. Even at half his age, he was the most powerful warlock in the world, save for Merlin himself, and many questioned even that. With that power came influence. It was a miracle really that he had consented to come to the Land of Shapeshifters to practice his arts, and King Kazar knew it.

Careful not to disturb the warlock, King Kazar trod lightly as he entered, in the gentlest of manners, but magic couldn't be fooled. A soft gibber carried through the room and warned the magic maker. Azhir lifted his head from his grimoire. "No need to explain yourself. I know why you're here."

King Kazar stopped with a huff, briefly offended that the warlock would expect him to justify his presence. "How do you know?" He couldn't help but reply. No one knew the thoughts of a king.

"The crow told me. He heard you give orders to your guard. You wish to see the progress of your gift." Azhir stole a glance at the dark fluttering of wings above them.

King Kazar stiffened. "I will not have you set your beasts to spy on me."

"They'll follow whom they choose," he said with an unbothered tone, "and share what they like." He picked up a wooden staff from against the stone wall and dusted it off. He waved it, and a blue crystal nested within it glowed brilliantly. A stir of air and dust whirled, and papers fluttered from the stacks of books. A gold crown encrusted with rubies, emeralds, and sapphires, soared between them. "I call it the Crown of Guilledon."

King Kazar gazed up at the glittering crown. The stones were simple and large, and the metal shined crudely. It was beautiful in its own way. "It's of the Western world," he noted tightly. He broke his gaze to meet the eyes of the warlock, wondering why he had chosen it as a gift for his brother.

"It is," agreed Azhir. "The borlaugs that forged it are of Cologne, from the Kingdom of the Franks. So naturally, it is of their world." He turned back to his grimoire, trailed his finger over the page, and scoured the spells. His eyes danced with hunger that no word seemed to satisfy, and so he continued scouring. "But I've made some adjustments."

"Adjustments?" King Kazar narrowed. Of course, Azhir, The Great Warlock of the East would have tinkered with the gift meant for his brother.

"Yes." Azhir looked up from his grimoire and smiled coyly.

"Aha! The real reason you took twice as long to prepare my gift. The truth reveals itself! You have been very secretive, and now I know why."

"Yes, and no," the warlock said, still entirely unperturbed, and King Kazar clenched at his arrogance. "Had this been an ordinary magic crown, the spells might have been simpler. As it is not, and it took longer to finish."

King Kazar waved his jeweled hand. He had heard the warlock's ramblings and complaints before and knew it all. The crown had been forged by borlaugs—terribly powerful beasts that hammer magic from the elements into the very cores of the chattels they create. And unable to wipe the crown of the borlaug's spells, Azhir had overlapped one enchantment with the next and then went back, carefully sewing them together. "I am aware of your troubles. That is why I'm compensating you so generously. What I was not aware of, was your additional tinkering."

King Kazar's gaze slid to the marvelous crown flickering above them. Only this warlock could have procured a rare piece of magic like this. Borlaugs turned junk into masterpieces. Even he, a non-wizard, knew that. A borlaug's magic was nameless. It couldn't be learned nor stolen. Only Azhir, The Great Warlock of The East, would have found a way around their enchantments.

"Would you like to see its power?"

"Why else would I, a king, set foot in a dreary dungeon like this?"

Azhir waved his staff. The crown drifted to him and rested gently on his palm. The moment it touched his skin, it transformed. The metal twisted and melted into a shimmering gold ribbon that flickered of a thousand colors in the soft light. It twirled and danced and spun into a beautiful, gold turban. Centered in the middle was the largest bloodstone King Kazar had ever seen. His breath escaped his lips.

"It's magnificent," he whispered. His gaze glittered with awe. It was the gift he had imagined for his brother. One worthy of uniting their kingdoms.

The warlock nudged the crown into the air, and it floated up between them, shifting back into the jewel-encrusted crown. When it had returned to its original position, he turned his wise look on the king. "It is a dangerous gift," he warned.

"It's dangerous for any magik to have the power of all magiks. But I trust my brother."

"Are you certain? Without any doubt, you trust the brother who left. The king who built the largest army across the magik kingdoms and conquered the lands of others?"

"If my brother were to understand the simplicities of shapeshifting—if he could know its power as I do—perhaps he would understand me better and accept our alliance," he entreated. "Maybe even, he will give up his pursuit of shadow walking." He chuckled half-heartedly.

"Or ... he will use the power you give him to take over your empire as he took the wizard's lands."

King Kazar stilled at the edge in the warlock's tone. It was true his brother had taken lands from other magik kingdoms and most recently, from the wizards. He conquered the first Island off the coast of Bilad al-Sham in a bloody battle. It was over the first night—before the sun rose. He attacked it unexpectedly in the cover of darkness before any help could come. His brother had known the wizards were run by a council that avoided war. So he took the next Island as well, known by the humans as Crete. Word of his conquests had spread like the wind and traveled as far as the sky breathes.

He pondered over the warlock's words. Though the warlock's reasoning was persuasive, he knew it came from a place of anger and resentment. Even if it was justified, he would not be fooled. "I will trust my brother. We grew up together, and he is my family."

"I thought as much." Azhir's voice snapped dryly. Fury entwined in the coarse sound. The firm set in his expression sharpened the bones in his cheeks, making them appear hollow and unforgiving. He straightened, making himself taller, and gathered his robes around him. "As I've said—I've made some adjustments, and I've added another spell."

"What spell?" King Kazar gritted lowly.

"One that will protect both our interests—too much is at stake. Not only your lands but the ones you promised to return in exchange for my magic—the ones stolen from the wizards."

King Kazar hated repeating himself. It was not something many would dare make a king do. Another proof of the warlock's daring. "What spell?" he asked tightly.

"If the King of the Shadowlands betrays you—if he were to overpower you or attempt to steal your kingdom—the crown will seize his will, chain his mind, and cloud his memories. He will forget his desire for power. And for as long as he wears the crown, his memories will fade, never lasting long enough to realize his mind is imprisoned. He will become magicless; unable to oppose you."

"*No,*" King Kazar thought.

"You will take his kingdom, lands, and titles, and with his army all that you desire will become yours."

"No," he whispered.

"The trolls will not be able to raid your lands. With your kingdoms aligned, your enemies will be outnumbered. Your reverence would be returned. Everything you've wished for will be yours."

"No," he shouted and then growled fiercely. "Remove the spell!" he said in a tone no one dared use when speaking to Azhir. It came out before he could control himself. And then it was too late, and he could not take it back.

Azhir's eyes twinkled dangerously. "It cannot be removed." He flicked his staff, and the crown spun. Dazzling light reflected off the stones. "It's sewn into the fabrics of the metal."

Riled by the warlock's obstinance, his face puffed up and he pointed his finger at a medallion caved in runes dangled against his chest. "I am king! You will remove it, or our agreement for the wizard lands is forfeit."

A glower shrouded Azhir. The cavern candles dampened with his mood, and the room went black. "Your word was given," his voice sounded in the flickering laboratory.

King Kazar forced his voice out evenly. "I promised the return of your lands peacefully—with the consent of my brother!"

"You promised the return of the lands for my assistance! With or without the shadow king's consent, you must return the lands of the wizards."

"No." King Kazar disagreed. He shook his head. This was not what he had wanted. He wanted to make peace with his brother. He wanted the old days to live again. And to show that, he wanted to bestow a crown, the most magnificent crown, as a gift. And Azhir had cursed it. Damn himself for trusting the warlock. "I want to do this the right way. I will convince King Zaeg to return the lands by his own will."

The fire in the candles brightened, and King Kazar could see again. Azhir tugged a metal bead knotted in his beard. "I can, perhaps, quiet the spell."

"Do it . . . and I will keep my word," King Kazar promised vehemently.

"As you wish."

The warlock threw back his head, and terror filled his face. His pupils blackened. A deep unnatural voice spoke though his lips did not move. The incantation echoed through the room. The lights did not return, and the floor shook. Stacked books tumbled over. Vials of liquid burst, one pop after another—

King Kazar covered his face from the shards. Then the sound was gone, and the cave was quiet. Bottles from all over the laboratory had exploded, and their remnants seeped together on the stone floor. "Did it work?" the king's voice shook.

Azhir wiped sweat before it trickled from his forehead, and he pointed his staff at the broken flasks and beakers. The staff glowed its deep crystalline hue, and the glass flew up. The sharp edges glittered dangerously and reassembled themselves, but the ruined potions didn't return. "The curse is contained—for now."

King Kazar forced his voice to steady. "What do you mean?"

"The crown will not act on its own if your brother betrays you. It will do nothing," he reiterated. "But," his voice hardened, "if he is not who you believe, and you cannot stop him, then you need only say these words to unlock the spell forever. The crown will take care of the rest." The warlock whispered in low tones, so soft the king couldn't hear him. But the words fluttered across the room like butterflies and spoke into his ear.

Amazed, King Kazar nodded slowly.

"Use them with care. Once spoken, they cannot be taken back."

A cool dread dampened the king's brow. "I understand."

Above them, a dark shadow crept through the crevices of the stone. It slithered down the shadowy walls, past the spilled potions, and slinked behind the warlock, tucking itself in a tight corner. It would have arrived sooner except the enchantments were hard to pass undeterred. But neither the king nor the warlock were aware of the intrusion, and that was worth the delay.

Azhir turned his attention to the spilt potions, now bubbling and smoking precariously. He swept his staff in the air. Crystal blue light erupted from the tip, and the hazardous potions lifted off the floor. "Venit," he commanded. Herbs and dried ingredients mobilized from scattered places and convened around the warlock. They danced around him, speaking to him, urging to be chosen. But ignoring their pleas, Azhir kept his gaze transfixed on the frothing elixir, and choosing his preferred ingredients, he calmed the volatile glop. Once it was done, he bottled the remnant and sealed it.

When all was quiet and the warlock was settled, the king cleared his throat. "May I test it?" He hesitated with his fingers stretched out. There were many powerful spells at work in the dungeon. He dared not do anything without consent from Azhir.

The warlock blinked up as if he had forgotten the king was there. "As you wish." He waved his staff, and the crown floated down and stopped in front of the king.

King Kazar plucked the sparkling crown from the air. The moment his fingers touched it, the heavy metal transformed. It molded, swirled, and dazzled, and a new turban formed. It was woven of blue silk with hundreds of pearls and lined with the blue stones of lapis, turquoise, and sapphire.

King Kazar sucked in a breath. "This is not the same as before."

"It is different for each hand that holds it," Azhir explained. "As are the virtues, desires, dreams, and vices."

King Kazar marveled at the turban and reverently placed it on his head. The turban retied itself magically.

Nothing happened. "What now?" the king puzzled.

"Use its magic," Azhir said, in his usual cryptic way.

"How?"

"You've seen your brother shadowshift? You must have some idea of what he does."

At this, the shadow tensed, condensing darkly, and two eyes, masked within the gloom, stared down astonishedly.

King Kazar thought of his brother, the tales of his transformations, and the strange experiments from when they were younger. He had seen it countless times and could picture his brother shadowshifting perfectly. His hands wisped away. His robes faded. And his flesh turned to shadows. The air around him became heavy and warm. And then, as if he'd done it a thousand times, he lept into the air and soared around the cave. He glided past a foggy orb, behind a casket of scrolls, between a dangling candelabra of fairy fire, and then landed in front of the eccentric warlock.

"Spectacular." King Kazar stared down at his billowing robes and gem-encrusted slippers, astonished by what he had done and that he was whole once again. He gathered his thoughts and removed the turban but kept it firmly in his grasp. "There are other treasures I can bestow upon my brother. I want to keep this for myself," he said, breathless.

Azhir smiled, amused. Then, seeing that King Kazar was serious, he waved his staff, and the turban was yanked from his grasp. "It was not fashioned for you. It is for the king of the Shadow Lands," he chastened. The turban soared back to its original place in the air above and transformed into the heavy gold crown. "The enchantments were spelled for your brother so that he may taste the power of shapeshifters and the power of all magiks."

King Kazar's eyes sparkled at the stones carved in the crude metal. "It's too powerful," he said softly. "I am giving him too much power."

"I believe I said something of the sort." Azhir mumbled. "I see that you weren't listening. But who listens to anyone who's right."

"I'm listening now." King Kazar continued to stare at the glittering gold. His eyes glazed over.

Azhir's keen eyes narrowed. "Without this gift, you may not be able to deliver your promise. I want the far lands of your brother's kingdom. You promised to return them to the wizards." His lip curled firmly.

The king tore his gaze from the crown. The Great Warlock of the East was right. This gift was created to reunite him with his brother. Without the gift to honor his brother, and prove his sincerity, their kingdoms may not unite. Trolls would set fire to his kingdom, and many would die. He would do anything to save his kingdom from such a fate.

"And you will have it," King Kazar swore.

The shadow twitched and jerked forward with vengeance—but Azhir's firm voice halted it. "If you don't return the lands of the wizards, your kingdom will face far more grievous enemies than you face now or any that you can imagine," warned Azhir. "You do not want me for an enemy," he said softly.

King Kazar sucked in air sharply and whirled to face the warlock. "You dare threaten your king?"

"You are not my king." Azhir held up a skull-ringed finger. "My allegiance is to my own. That is the way of magiks. Your expansions and invasions—constantly trying to transcend your brother—have taken what belongs to my brothers. I want it returned," he finished firmly.

"I gave you my word, and I will see it done." Offended and afraid of how far he had taken his words with the great warlock, King Kazar stomped for the arduous stairs that led back to the fresh air he craved. He was not stupid enough to challenge Azhir, but his patience was spent, and the dark cave was dampening his mood. As he reached the door, the warlock's voice halted him.

"Don't forget the words," warned Azhir. "Exactly as I said them."

Remembering the whispered chant, the king shivered, and his blood turned cold. "I could not, even if I wanted."

Chapter Four
A Jinn's Way

King Zaeg

Not many moments passed after King Kazar left, that the laboratory became uncomfortably quiet. Not a frog croaked, nor a raven cawed, nor a mouse stirred. It was like the books, walls, and residue of magic wished to betray the intruder. A heavy unease hung in the room. There were no sounds. It was so starkly different from moments before when the clamorous King was present, that it was like no sound existed at all. And soon the warlock went to making his own noise, just to settle the nerves that were stirring.

Amidst the clacking and racking as the warlock busied about, something else roused in the corner of the dungeon. The shadow stretched. First testing that the warlock was not alerted, and then seeing he was not, it slipped out from the cranny and enveloped the ceiling in darkness. Deep within the shadow, King Zaeg shuddered with fury. *Treachery! Everywhere I turn—treachery! My brother intends to gift me this crown, and once I feel like we are brothers again, convince me to give away the wizard isles. Those lands supply my army with ore and steel. They are full of magic stones that sell for gold. I depend on them to feed my kingdom. And my brother must remember that anything he asked of me as children, I granted. Family takes care of family.*

King Zaeg fought back another wave of fury. The more his brother's words played in his head, the more unstable his wrath became. And when he was angry, it was difficult to stay hidden.

He inhaled deeply and let the air out. His shadow brushed against the crown dangling beneath him. The metal was cool and moist, and it tingled against him. He twisted to face it, curiously. *Strong enchantments are the only thing that feel like that in my shadow form,* he told himself. He dipped lower so that he was inches from the large, crude gems. *My brother said its power was too great to give away, even to me, his brother.* He circled the crown, suspended by nothing but magic. *Then my brother used it to shadowshift. Something I never thought I would see. It must be incredibly powerful, and power can be dangerous when not understood. Hmm.* He shied away, giving it more space. As he circled the jeweled crown an intense desire to possess it grew. *Perhaps, since my brother will use it to manipulate me, or even keep it for himself, I should just take it now. I will find another wizard to help me understand it...*

"Why aren't you gibbering?" Azhir craned his ear to the side and called out to the mice, "The spell is finished. The king of shapeshifters is gone."

The room remained silent.

Azhir flicked his wrist, annoyed. "Ah, bother. Do what you will." But even as he disregarded his pets, he scrunched his nose and waited for noise to fill the room again. In the silence, a knowing gleam sparkled in his eye. "Unless . . . we aren't alone?"

A chill prickled through King Zaeg, and he recoiled against the ceiling. He could not escape with the crown now. Azhir would discover him if he lingered any longer, and the warlock was not one to quarrel with. Without wasting another moment, he slipped through the watery cracks of the laboratory and headed back through the tunnels. At the surface, the ground was met with fields as far as one could see. Rays of fiery orange streaked across the sky. His brother had not gone very far. He strolled leisurely as he watched the sun set behind the palace. Soon the celebration would begin.

"My King!" Firoza called. She led a small command of soldiers that clambered behind her with their swords drawn. Her face was flushed, and her voice was tense. "One of our search parties has captured a raider—a desert troll."

King Kazar snapped up from his peaceful daze. "It will be to his death."

Firoza caught up to him and knelt. Her distress was obvious, and it brought King Zaeg closer, until he was just above them, hidden beneath a shadow cast from a giant oak.

"That is not all, My King," she said with her head bent and her eyes on the ground. "The troll brought a jinni with him. The two alone have destroyed an entire outpost. My spies say they've moved on to a neighboring village just south of the first."

"Where did the trolls find a jinni?" King Kazar exclaimed, his tone tense. It was obvious to King Zaeg that his brother was struggling to process the news. But he was used to war, and attacks no longer surprised him.

"We're not sure. The troll is dead. I believe the jinni is making its way here."

King Kazar motioned for her to rise. "Are you certain of the troll's death?"

Firoza signaled, and one of her soldiers brought forward a bloodied club. "This was taken from his corpse. The villagers fought bravely."

"Where are my scouts?" he demanded. "They should have reported this immediately."

"They're dead."

King Kazar clutched his chest, and he whipped around wildly. A gasp softened his words, "It's begun."

Firoza squared her shoulders and attempted to reassure him. "We've already sent reinforcements. I recommend another battalion leave at once. We'll need Azhir for the jinni. I fear he is the only one that can defeat it."

"Dare I ask, what kind of jinni?"

Firoza paused as if she wished not to say. "My spies say it is a Marid."

King Kazar startled abruptly and whipped towards the palace balcony. A soft light flickered in the window. "Who is guarding my brother?" he groused and whirled on Firoza. "You were commanded to keep watch!"

Firoza's wings fluttered as she dipped her head in another bow. "Forgive me. I've lost him."

"What do you mean? We cannot lose him. It's too dangerous!" he nearly shouted.

"I stood guard outside his chamber. He did not leave, nor did anyone enter, through that door. But a servant brought up his belongings and found the room empty."

"Were there injuries?" King Kazar's voice scratched.

"There was no sign of a struggle," she replied.

"Nor would there be." King Kazar's shoulders slumped slightly. "My brother was never one to stay where he was told. Send someone to find him and someone else to collect Azhir. Meanwhile, gather as many fighters as possible. Then, send an envoy to alert the captain at the border. His brigade will stay to defend the palace. We will meet the jinni at the village and stop him there."

Firoza gestured to her soldiers, and two hurried off in opposite directions.

MAGIKS AND THE TALE OF TWO KINGS

King Zaeg drifted lower on the scene transpiring beneath him. A small grin still pressed on his lips. It was true that he never did stay where he was told. His brother remembered him well. But the smile faded as the seriousness of the situation settled in.

After what he'd heard in the warlock's dungeon, he would've left his brother to face the invader alone, but a loose jinni was a serious matter. His brother may be traitorous, but this kingdom once belonged to his father. Besides, these lands neighbored his own. If the jinni wasn't dealt with here, it could come for his kingdom next. It was best to face the danger before it destroyed any of his own villages. He pushed his anger and the lost hope of reuniting with his brother deep inside. With no reason left to hide, King Zaeg shadowshifted, and he appeared from the darkness.

The flash of surprise in King Kazar's face was quickly smothered. "You haven't changed a bit."

King Zaeg's eyes twinkled. He forced back his anger and met his brother's eyes. "I hear you have a jinni loose in your kingdom."

King Kazar snorted. But he didn't ask how long his brother had been eavesdropping. "I do."

"I'll help you purge it from our father's lands. You'll need the fighters I brought with me to defeat him," he said proudly.

King Kazar nodded solemnly. Everyone knew of the skill of the shadow walker soldiers. Many called them assassins.

King Zaeg beckoned one of Firoza's soldiers forward. He was lean, and his trained muscles suggested he was fast. King Zaeg whispered, and the soldier hurried off in the direction of the palace. As expected, it wasn't long before his regiment of shadow assassins appeared around him, armed with daggers and swords and dressed in black. The Shadow Land's emblem shone on their breasts.

King Kazar raised a brow. It wasn't unnoticed that the shadow walkers returned first, appearing out of nothingness, though the shapeshifter soldiers had a head start. King Zaeg saw his brother's displeasure, and his lip curled to the side humorously. But soon the shapeshifters marched in, dressed in vibrant, regal red, and King Kazar turned to Firoza. "Lastly, we need Azhir. Where is he?"

"I'm here," Azhir materialized with first his nose, then his slippers and garments, and bit by bit, the rest of him. He stood as aloof as ever, his robes swaying with the breeze. "I've been searching for a jinni for a very long time."

King Kazar turned to the warlock, but what he was going to say was lost. A frown formed and puckered in disgust. "Azhir, your eyes . . . they're missing!"

"They're not missing," Azhir said, unconcernedly. His empty gaze drank in the night. "I know exactly where they are."

Seeing the empty black sockets, King Zaeg's stomach turned. "Where are they then?" he managed.

"Where I put them," the warlock said simply.

"But don't you need them?" insisted King Kazar.

"Of course. They're waiting for me in the village. I would have sent my ears too, but I prefer them here at the moment."

"Is the village okay?" King Kazar asked with an ominous tone that suggested he knew the answer.

"On the contrary, it is very bad." The warlock paused and stared off into nothingness like he could see something they could not. "There is not a jinni."

"There is not?" King Kazar repeated, breathless.

"There are two," Azhir replied, and the words rang heavy in the air.

A sharpness in King Kazar's voice stung the silence. "What do we do?"

Azhir scratched his chin. "We defeat the weaker jinni first. I will trap the stronger one when he is outnumbered."

"Azhir," Firoza voiced gravely, "this is not the time to capture magic for your laboratory."

"As a master, I must always be a student. As a student, I must always strive to master."

King Kazar forced a cough, covering the awkwardness. He turned to a decorated soldier in his rank, with graying hair and a wide jawline. "General Harun, what would you say?"

"Kill it," the general's sneer curled his lip over a scar in the corner of his mouth. "Kill them both and save the lives they'd take if we didn't."

King Zaeg stayed quiet. He was keen on the scene unfolding before him. It surprised him that his brother had not immediately consented to the request of The Great Warlock of the East. Instead, he had given his general a say. Perhaps King Kazar had become accustomed to Azhir and his strange ways. If he had, then the familiarity clouded his judgement. They could not defeat the jinn alone.

Azhir exhaled slowly. He chose his next words with deliberation. "The knowledge of jinn is scarce. I have yet to encounter a jinni, and I may not have another opportunity. Therefore, if you want my help, we will capture one of the two." His words rang with the threat of facing the jinn alone, and King Zaeg was not surprised by it.

"Fine," King Kazar consented, having no other choice.

"My King, the horses were freed in the field," General Harun said gruffly, masking his dissatisfaction with the decision. "It's a half-day's ride to the village. We may not arrive in time to save it."

"Perhaps, I have a way." Azhir lifted his staff. Blue sparkles dazzled from the tip. He muttered, and thunder clapped in the sky. The ground beneath them shook, frightening the soldiers, and they scrambled to catch their footing. A hole opened in the earth, and a herd of nearly hairless beasts galloped from within. Each had a curved horn, with a wispy mane, and a tuft of hair at the end of their tail. There was one for every two magiks, though each beast was large enough to hold three fully armored fighters. Light glittered above their forelocks, flickered down their jowls, and dazzled around their muzzles. The sparkle settled and formed sturdy, leather trappings.

"Karkadann," muttered King Zaeg. His eyes shone at the mystical creatures. Whispers spread across the field. They all had believed Karkadann were extinct. King Zaeg believed it too. He had given up his search years ago. His father, the Great King, had owned one. Its lineage had been traced back to the Persian King Xerces, but his father had failed to find it a mate, and no one had seen one since.

King Zaeg barely noticed his own footsteps as he closed the distance to a particularly large male that shimmered under the rising moon. His fingers brushed its black, leathery skin. The beast brayed and bumped its head eagerly. But Azhir was the first to mount.

A silvery female with intelligent eyes and a proud gait approached the warlock, perhaps by choice or by magic. Fumbling, he climbed atop the beast, worse than any recruit that ever joined his ranks, and with the warlock's encouragement, the two kings and then the soldiers mounted. When all the soldiers were seated, the Karkadann took off, steered by the warlock and his gleaming staff.

The strides of the Karkadann were fluid and smooth. The thunderous gallop of their golden hooves carried like a storm across the fields, but there were no imprints. It was like they never existed, nor traipsed across the fields. What should have taken hours, took only minutes. For time froze, and space aligned with golden strings of magic. The Karkadann roped the distance with these lassos of light and pulled themselves ahead of space before time started again.

At the outskirts of the village, their beasts slowed, and the strings of light disappeared. The once bustling village was a haunted wasteland. Rubble and decay dirtied the starlit mountain village, and ash polluted the sky. The sight cooled the warm magic of the Karkadann and broke the soldiers from their trance. The scent of death hung at the entrance of two pillars. Red streaks of blood stained the gates, and beyond that, a blackness awaited, promising demise.

Azhir steered his Karkadann up beside the two kings. He mumbled a rhythm of words. Some were of the old tongue, and others were never heard before. His crystal staff glowed deeper, almost black, like the dark magic he conjured. The hollow pits, where his eyes should be, glistened, and black ink trickled from the empty holes. A flash of light sped from within the gates, illuminating the blackness that hung over the village. It blurred between the soldiers, and struck the warlock in the face, nearly dismounting him.

Azhir grunted roughly. He grabbed his mount to steady himself. "I never liked this part," he said with one empty socket and one eyeball that teared. "But it seems to be the only way," he regretted, and even as he said it, a second light came from behind, curved around his head, and struck him from an angle that must have hurt dreadfully.

The two kings were stunned into a reverent silence. They waited, uncertain of how to respond, as the warlock smeared the tears and black ink from his cheeks.

"Shall we?" Azhir gathered his reins and steered his beast. The soldiers cleared a path for him, and he led the way through the gated posts.

Inside the gates, cries echoed from deep within the darkness. A blaze of fire overtook the sky. Bodies lay in puddles of their own blood. It was fear that kept the soldiers astride their magical beasts, and everyone felt it. King Zaeg looked on the village in horror.

He steered his Karkadann closer to his brother's. "Keep our beasts together so that we can protect our backs."

Without a word, King Kazar nodded.

Most of the trek through the village was silent and undisturbed. Only the scent of death stirred until they reached the center, where above a hut, was not a man, nor a beast, but a jinni.

Battered shields from fallen warriors were bent into a collar that adorned his neck. His piercings were made of bone. Gold cuffs wielded his wrists. His torso was bare, and he floated above a wisp of smokeless fire that swirled in a cyclone. It licked the air around it and vaporized an ill-fortuned sandgrouse that had gotten caught in the wind and was drawn beneath it. But it was the hate that glowered in his smirk, and his intelligent gaze, that was frightening.

Behind the jinni, a cloud of sand and dirt swirled unnaturally. It crumbled rooftops as it tore through the sky.

"This is worse than I thought," murmured King Kazar.

"The village is beyond saving," replied King Zaeg.

Azhir whispered but the soft words traveled like the wings of a butterfly so that all the soldiers heard him, "The bearded man is Marid, the strongest of the jinn. The storm is his companion, Jann. Jann is the first of the jinn and the weakest of all that came after."

"LEAVE THIS PLACE," King Kazar's voice shook. "Never return to the Land of Shapeshifters!"

Marid's bearded chin puckered. His ebony eyes narrowed as he assessed the soldiers. A thick wrinkle folded across his forehead. "You sought us out?" He threw his head back in a laugh that boomed. It shook the pebbles beneath them, and the soldiers covered their ears in surprise. Only the stubborn ones held firm, so as not to appear weak.

Behind Madrid, the storm curled under itself like dust that stirred from the hooves of a thousand Arabian horses. The storm picked up speed, giving a glimpse of the night sky before it swallowed the heavens again.

"You have offended Jann," a deep voice broke from Madrid. He smiled, but not with kindness. Wickedness curled in his lips, and blood blotted the gaps of his teeth.

Several gasps sounded amongst the soldiers. Bravery turned to disgust, and fear shined in their eyes like dying flickers of candlelight.

King Zaeg recognized the spreading fear, and he pulled the reins of his Karkadann around to face them. "Do not fear the demons before you. They do not own the sky or the land. They were created, and all that are born can perish. If judgement has not yet come for their ghastly deeds, then judgement is what we bring tonight!" His Karkadann riled beneath him, and shouts rang from the soldiers.

General Harun whispered to King Kazar and then used the attention King Zaeg had gathered to deliver his command, "Shapeshifters distract Madrid! Shadow soldiers attack Jann, the weaker of the jinn!"

King Zaeg grimaced. No one had ever dared give orders to his own soldiers without first consulting him. He wondered what the general had whispered. Perhaps Harun had asked permission from his own king? It appeared that way. Then why did he send the shadow walkers after Jann instead of Madrid?

His soldiers were the best fighters in the world, and Jann was the weakest of the jinn. He would let the insolence slide, for now. It was the warlock's plan to defeat Jann first, and they had agreed to it. His soldiers would defeat Jann and show the shapeshifter army what real magic was.

The moment passed to reprimand the general, and Harun sprinted forward with ferocity that was catching. "Death to the jinn!" he roared. Battle cries filled the air. Soldiers drove their heels into the bellies of their Karkadann, and the ground rumbled as they galloped into the fight. King Kazar and Firoza, the captain of his guard, rode with them.

King Zaeg leapt up on the back of his Karkadann and lurched into the sky. He soared, feeling the lightness of the air around him, and then shadowshifted. He swirled around the cyclone of smokeless flames, and the heat from the blaze tickled his shadow. Heat did not hurt him as it did the shapeshifters. It was in the laws of magic—the laws that his brother knew but were lost beneath the other shining qualities of shapeshifting that he favored.

Azhir did not follow the kings. He dismounted and raised his staff to the sky. His voice started low, softer than a whisper, for whispers can be heard. At the end of each rhythm of his hum, his voice grew.

Madrid laughed at the shapeshifters riding towards him. "If you want to attack me, you have to get past Jann first."

Jann circled around and descended on the two armies. Before they could attack, he blew them back like a mighty tornado. Soldiers hurled through the sky, and in one gust, both armies were scattered.

Azhir got caught in a strong gale of wind. In his shadow form, he could not fight the speed and strength behind it, and the wind carried Azhir into the fields. He landed lightly in tall blades of wheat, far from his shadow soldiers. He hurried to regroup and lead them in the next attack. As he soared, he saw his brother leading the shapeshifter army.

"Shapeshifters! Secure yourselves from the wind!" King Kazar cried. He leapt from his Karkadann and shapeshifted. His limbs took root in the ground. They twisted and grew and anchored deep beneath the soil. Branches sprouted from his arms, and at a safe distance from the heat, he hurled stones at Madrid.

The wind punched his chest and hurled at his limbs, ripping them apart. Never had King Zaeg seen his brother in pain such as this, as the air tore at his trunk and snatched oak leaves from his fingertips. But his brother pushed his wooded roots out and grew. Once he was as tall as the sky, he swung his branches at Jann, but Jann was everywhere, and the tree did not hurt him.

"Hahahahaa," Madrid laughed from deep in his belly. "You think you are a match for Jann?" He smirked at the disarrayed soldiers and King Kazar's failed attack.

Azhir's chant amplified. The verse resonated over the storm. The words rang clear like crystal, yet the moment they were heard, they were forgotten.

As Madrid and Jann were unfamiliar with a talented warlock, and they had only crossed paths with primitive and crude magic, they only paused for a moment. Jann was the first to attack the maker of words.

Gusts of wind blew in unexpected angles. The sky darkened, and two giant fists formed in the storm. They pulled air into the whirlwind, and the storm grew. The shadow army was closest, and they threw their swords and daggers at Jann. The whirl of wind pulled them in, and they vanished. A gaping mouth opened in the middle of the storm.

"Find cover!" cried King Zaeg, but it was too late.

Air, debris, huts, and broken timber were sucked into it. Jann dragged King Zaeg's best soldiers from the sky and consumed them in his gaping mouth. And just as the storm was bigger than the king's palace, Jann blew.

Whoosh. Loud and thunderous wind hurled the debris, daggers, and bodies back at the shapeshifter army. The two kinds of changers tumbled over one another as dead shadow walkers were spewed onto shapeshifters. King Zaeg watched in horror, unable to save his shadow army. Jann sucked in more air, ready to deliver the final blow that would destroy them all.

Azhir tapped the ground with his staff. A rippling wave of power trembled through the earth. It split the earth's crust from his staff to the middle of Jann. The windstorm was speared and thrusted off-course. Madrid's smokeless flames were snuffed, and his laughter cut off abruptly.

For one long moan of wind, there was silence.

The two kings gazed upon the wreckage. What was left of the village was destroyed. There was nothing but an empty stretch of farming field that led to the snowcapped mountains, where the trolls were known to come. In the swaying stalks of wheat were a strew of bodies that Jann had regurgitated.

General Harun lay dead, along with half a dozen shapeshifters. The shapeshifter army had anchored themselves in the ground, and for that, were mostly unharmed. Few had cuts and bruises, but nearly all survived Jann's assault. Meanwhile, the shadow soldiers, who attacked Jann head-on, had been sacrificed.

Cries of anguish filled King's Zaeg's ears. Heavy tears glossed his eyes. He had loved his fighters and devoted his life to training them. Spending day after day honing their skills, they learned to trust one another. They had formed a close friendship. Their trust and camaraderie along with their skill had made them the fiercest warriors across the lands.

He wiped a smudge of dirt from his face. Moisture puddled his lashes, and his eyes burned. He squeezed them tightly. A thick tear cooled his skin and ran down his cheek. His gaze traveled across his dead fighters and landed on his own captain. His breath turned heavy, and the urge to drag himself to his friend's side was overwhelming. But he couldn't lift himself to do it. His gaze raked over his captain hoping he may still be alive. But the captain laid still, and his eyes did not blink.

King Zaeg cried out, and when the curdling wail died, he tore his gaze across the battlefield. The sight curled his lip in anger. *How fortunate for my brother that his army lives while my own is obliterated.* Anger twisted in his gut. He kneeled over and fell to the ground. He held his stomach as the pain clenched and burned. *I wish I had not answered my brother's call. Had I known the fate that awaited us I never would have come. Not for a brother whose words are filled with lies and deceit.*

Chapter Five
The Shadow's Choice

Azhir, The Great Warlock of the East

The wind was still. The breeze did not blow, and the storm did not howl, but the hem of the warlock's robe rippled and flowed as it would with a strong draft. He had needed more time to weave enough power in his enchantment. But if he had waited, Jann would have crushed the soldiers in the last attack. He had made a quick decision and cast the unfinished spell. One more attack from Jann would have killed them all. As tempting as it would be to let a blow weaken the changers, it could not be done. Not for the balance of magic to remain stable.

His pride steered his thoughts to the outcome where he would have to face the jinn alone. One warlock against the vast power of two ancient beings. The thought tickled in his belly and bubbled up in his chest. A smile formed on his lips. His spells would be faster of course. They had to be. And he would not have been able to spare one of the jinn in order to capture it. But he would have won. His grin spread. The battle would have been told for centuries, and the wizards would have chronicled his conquest in the towering library with the greatest histories of wizards. And with the shadow army depleted, there wouldn't be enough strength for the shadow kingdom to stop the wizards from taking back their homelands. He would've gotten exactly what King Kazar had promised in the beginning, and he would have tested his power against a worthy foe.

But alas, no. He could not let the kingdoms of changers fall. Not either of them. They kept balance in the world of magiks. If the King of Shapeshifters fell here, the trolls would come down from the mountains in masses and overrun the lands. The elves and fairies would go to war for the scraps left by the trolls, and then eventually they would all war together. It would bring more death to the wizards, one way or another.

The fire beneath Madrid forged and curled. It kindled, even after the anoxia from his hex. Now that his enchantment had fizzled out, Jann's winds blew softly. His unfinished spell had not extinguished the storm. It had only quieted it.

Madrid righted himself. Anger splashed red across his high cheekbones. The crimson color spread to the flat span of his forehead, then to the point of his chin, so that his face was bright with fury. In his fury, he shrank. He shrank until he was not larger than the Karkadann. His torso hovered above a swirl of heat that seared the shrubs beneath it.

Thunder clapped, and Jann whipped in the sky.

"Ready yourselves!" King Kazar cried from his mount. His soldiers pounded their palms against their armor, and the clang echoed across the field.

But Madrid ignored them and turned his fiery gaze on Azhir. His eyes shrank to slits.

Azhir drew a quick rune around him and his Karkadann. The intricate design burned in the grass and illuminated, and a cool barrier sealed him from the battle. Protected, Azhir began the next incantation, slightly different than the first. He spun one spell over another. Though his thoughts were focused on the spell, all that passed and was spoken came into his web, so that he knew and heard all that transpired.

Firoza centered herself amongst the riders and speared her fist in the air. "Right-wing—spread east. Left-wing—fall back!"

The Karkadann clopped into the stream, and the army repositioned. With General Harun dead, she was in command, and the fate of the soldiers depended on her.

Azhir had long believed the fairy should lead the shapeshifter army. She was far more cunning than any of the other councilmen and soldiers King Kazar kept in his inner circle. It was the king's regard for her safety that kept her from leading his army into battle and safely close by his side. Already, the army's positioning was much better protected, and that would give him the time he needed.

"Attack!" Firoza cried.

Madrid drew a sword from the air as if the sky was his scabbard. His first strike split the closest shapeshifter in two. His second cut down a Karkadann. His third sliced through both the shield and armor of an unwitting soldier. Each slash was swift and precise, and Madrid left a strew of bodies in one breath. He drew closer to Azhir and the shapeshifter king and swung his sword through the air.

Firoza dug her heels into the belly of her beast and pushed her Karkadann through the platoon. Her hoarse voice choked out more orders, and she changed her tactics again. "Shieldguard—protect the king!" She signaled for another unit to outflank the jinni. "Nightguard—rear blitz!"

Soldiers scrambled to attack from behind, while King Zaeg kneeled on the battlefield, surrounded by the bodies of his shadow walkers. He had not moved since they had fallen. Even from the edge of the field, Azhir could feel his agony. The pulsing grief was drawn into his web, and it clashed with the unfolding scenes on the field of battle.

The king of shapeshifters will need his brother's help against Madrid, he told himself. He gently waved his staff in the shadow king's direction, and a sparkle of blue drizzled on his shoulders.

King Zaeg let out a throaty wail, giving wind to his anger. As Azhir removed his pain, rage filled the emptiness in his chest. His cry turned to a gut-wrenching screech. When there was no more wind in his breath, he turned his black eyes on his brother and then the jinni. He let out a slow breath, turned into a shadow, and disappeared from the warlock's view. "This will all end soon," he promised.

That the king of shadows had vanished without a trace, bothered Azhir. It was a dangerous disadvantage that could not be ignored. He wondered if there had been other times that the shadow had crept around the palace without his notice. And if other shadow walkers had learned the same illusion. If they had, it could be very bad for the wizards. He would dabble in his ancient texts when he returned to his laboratory, but meanwhile, he turned his attention back to the battle.

Firoza drew thin metal blades from her braided hair. She steadied her boots in the unkept weeds and crouched into a spring. The muscles in her back flexed, and her fairy wings spread out. As her soldiers attacked, so did she. Only a flicker of light against the steel knives could be seen as her blades flew at the jinni.

Madrid drew a shield from the air. Almost simultaneously, he blocked Firoza's knives. One. Two. Three. The fourth slipped under his arm and caught him in the side. "Aaah," he bellowed. He cut down the next soldier and turned his path for the king.

Firoza threw another round of knives. As they approached their target, she unhooked fairy discs from her armguards and threw those too. The knives were deflected, but the discs were not. They dug deep into Madrid's collarbone and got stuck in his shoulder blades.

"Gaaah!" Madrid screamed and dropped his swords. He reached for his back where the blades stuck through and unable to grab them, pulled them out with magic. He bellowed in pain. When they were free, he shot Firoza a murderous glare.

Firoza responded with another round of discs.

Madrid lept in the air and landed in front of her, killing the soldiers guarding her instantly. He drew a new blade and slashed at her chest. Had it been another soldier, he would have taken his last breath, but Firoza countered. She stumbled back from the impact and adjusted her stance.

Azhir quickened his spell as Firoza and Madrid broke into a fierce sword battle. Centuries of honing his skill delivered Madrid the upper hand. He learned her strikes and counters and quickly took the lead in their dance. He feigned a strike—used a soft counter to draw her in close—and swung hard where her defense was weak.

"Aah!" King Kazar blocked the strike meant for Firoza, and for the second time, Firoza barely escaped death. She shifted her weight to her toes and attacked again.

Madrid drew a second sword, one for the king and one for Firoza, but the swords were heavy and meant for two-armed attacks. Sweat trickled down his brow, and his strikes became unsteady.

Above them, the windstorm howled. Finally having gathered enough strength, Jann circled in the sky to help tip the odds back in the Jinn's favor. Debris clattered as the storm picked the rubble up again.

Azhir drew another rune. Soft steam rose from the magic he padded in the air. He swung his staff, releasing a full and overflowing spell. His chant burst forth. The sound boomed. Words with meanings unknown to changers stampeded like the hooves of a thousand Arabian mounts. Soldiers across the battlefield covered their ears as the words pierced the storm with a powerful song. The collision cracked. Thunder rumbled. And Jann was trapped. His wind raged against a cage that wove around him. Beyond it, there was not the softest breeze.

A shadow dimmed the moonlit glow above. King Kazar gathered the last of his stamina. Together, he and Firoza struck Madrid—Madrid countered, kicked Firoza in the stomach, and swung King Kazar's fatal blow—

A muffled pierce squelched behind him. His swing halted. His grip slacked, and the sword clattered to the ground. He reached for his stomach, where a blade stuck through. A pained breath escaped his lips. "No," Madrid garbled.

The blade shoved deeper, and it tore a gash in Madrid's chest. Blood gurgled free, and he fell to his knees. "Ngh!" he exhaled sharply.

Behind him stood King Zaeg with his hand on the hilt. He pulled the blade free and threw it on the ground with disgust. His furious eyes turned on Firoza. Her chest heaved under her jeweled armor. She had fought honorably. His gaze turned and landed on his brother. Light scratches and matted blood covered King Kazar's arms and chest, but he was whole and in better shape than the rest. Azhir could see that it angered the king of shadow walkers. There was a lingering spark of fury and curl of disgust in his lips that did not fade when finding that his brother had survived the assault. Rather he glared as though he wished to draw a sword against King Kazar himself, and just as it piqued the warlock's interest, the look was gone.

"You saved us!" exclaimed King Kazar. His voice burned proudly. "You defeated the jinni!" His tone changed and pitched excitedly. "That trick! When did you learn to hide so stealthily? Even I did not sense you."

King Zaeg turned his back on his brother and looked over the field. He sucked in a shallow breath, and sorrow poured from his eyes. Tears leaked down his cheeks, blurring his vision. "I saved you, but not my army," he choked.

"Come now. Don't blame yourself. You will train new fighters." King Kazar attempted to console him and patted his shoulder.

"And what of my friends? Will I replace them so easily?"

King Kazar's response was spared by a cry from the last jinni. It blew with the wind and lamented against the snare of magic that restrained him.

Azhir's rhythmic chant that had thundered across the fields, was now soft, and it crooned like a lullaby. He could feel the fight draining from Jann as his curse sucked the air from the storm. Jann was not the jinni he had intended to capture, but sometimes fate chooses your path for you.

His words spun in a soft tune, and he left them suspended in the air. They shrouded the night sky, like the heavy mist after a thunderstorm. Jann was a mere overcast now. Drizzling rain and soft winds blew against a web of magic that entrapped him and shrank with each passing heartbeat. Soon the jinni would fit into one of the bottles that dangled from his belt, and if he raged against the curse none would know.

"It's over!" whispered King Kazar.

Zrooom. A light shot across the sky. Crack. It snapped against the magic prison. The clap muffled the soft note of magic, and the light exploded the cage. Bang!

When the explosion of magic settled, Azhir searched the clear span of the unclouded canopy. Jann had escaped, and it was Madrid that had sent a final blast of magic setting him free.

A low grumble rolled across the land. A sudden crack pealed, and a single bolt of lightning streaked through the midnight sky. Azhir conjured a shield in the last fleeting second. Lightning exploded off the protective barrier. The force knocked him back, and he fell against his Karkadann. Screams echoed as Jann soared free, and a tumultuous thunderstorm blocked the orange sunrise that tinted the horizon. Lightning crackled. The storm surged, and the air turned electric.

"We're all in one place," King Kazar murmured. "He is going to wipe out our entire army at once!" he screamed.

Firoza shoved a soldier next to her. "Spread out!" She curled her wings and took flight. "Spread out!" she cried, and the soldiers trampled over one another to get out of the way of the storm.

Azhir picked himself up and patted his Karkadann. "Thank you, friend," he said to the beast, and then he added, though more to himself, "Jann is more powerful than I thought." *No matter. I will change the design of my spell. If sound can drown out my tune, then I'll blow magic without sound. Where strength is not needed, wit brings triumph.*

He thumped his staff against the dirt. Magic dazzled blue. An indigo bead formed at the tip. It grew from a seed to a bud and blossomed. The petals wilted, and the seeds whisked into the air. Magic carried them into the wind. Like tuffs of a dandelion, they blew with the breeze. The staff continued to spell seeds, and soon the storm was full of fluffy pappuses of enchanted words without sound.

Just another few moments and Jann will be trapped. Azhir smiled to himself. *He will not be able to break this enchantment, as there is no song for the wind to drown out.*

Just as Azhir thought it, the winds shifted abruptly, and the clouds curled underneath. Before he could discern the change, Jann fled! "No," Azhir murmured, and the sky carried the sound across the battlefield. There was a moment of hesitation amongst the soldiers, but as the confusion faded, cheers erupted. Madrid was dead—and Jann had fled!

Azhir smothered his disappointment. *There is little knowledge of the jinn,* he reminded himself. *I have much to learn.* He bunched the bridle in his fist and mounted his Karkadann. "Are you ready for an adventure?" he asked and steered the mythical creature towards the two kings.

It was a few long strides, and Azhir tugged lightly on the reins, pulling the silvery Karkadann to a stop amidst the circle of shapeshifters cheering around their king. Frustration still pinched in King Zaeg's features, but Azhir had not the time to uncover his irritation. "I will return shortly," he said brusquely.

"Jann is cleverer than I thought. Perhaps more than Madrid who overpowered him." *He may be tricky to catch,* he thought to himself, and then added, "Perhaps a fortnight or two—if fate is on my side."

Azhir steered his beast around them, but King Kazar stepped in his path. "The Kingdom is facing too great a danger. We need you here."

Azhir frowned. Years of schooling, under the greatest wizards in the world, and yet, extraordinarily little knowledge of the jinn was gathered. Even the oldest grimoires left unfinished pages where the powers and histories should be scribed. How could he explain that to a shapeshifter who had never been taught by the wizards. He opened his mouth to try and King Kazar interrupted him.

"We need to ensure the safety of these lands," insisted Kazar—the shapeshifter who would have him call him king.

Azhir grimaced. Though he cared little for the crumbling brotherhood between the two kings, he did care about the likelihood of war if the kingdom of shapeshifters fell. Yet King Kazar would never understand the remarkable power slipping away. "You ask too much." His lips tightened resolutely. He had done what he could. He had created the crown. His magic had stopped the jinn.

"And return yours," King Kazar mumbled softly.

Azhir's grip on his reins tightened. His teeth clenched. "I will stay a little longer." His eyes wandered past Kazar, to his brother's stricken gaze, and then to the trail of destruction. A gleam hardened in the corners of his eyes. "Don't waste the time I give you. I will leave while the trail is fresh."

Chapter Six
The King's Fallacy

King Kazar

The celebration was postponed. Too many were dead to return with the bodies, and their graves were dug in the fields. Mostly they were shadow walkers. *But that is because shapeshifting is a better evolution of magic,* King Kazar told himself. Maybe now, his brother would see it.

The remaining Karkadann returned from where they came. Azhir barely spoke, but he tapped his staff, the ground opened up, and the Karkadann dove inside without a trace that they ever existed.

It had been a full day that the palace slept. For if the king slept, then so did his guests, as they should, and as he commanded. All slept, except the servants, who set to work like a bouquet of warblers foraging in the pre-dawn sun. They busied about with grateful hearts. For if the two kings would save a distant village on the far border of the mountain pass then surely they would save the kingdom from trolls.

By evening, the tale of the defeated jinn had spread, and the servants had prepared a noble feast. Music and laughter drifted through the palace. The smells of mutton and saffron carried through the halls. Impatient to join the festivities and settle the matter of the troll invasion with his brother, King Kazar hurried through the final hour. He dressed in his finest robes; a soft linen ghilala, an exquisite silk qamis, a stately qaba crafted of rich brocade, and a high court mantle made of silk and gold thread.

He ushered his servants from his chamber and shapeshifted into his usual guise. His body shrank, his vision adjusted to the nightfall, and he grew scruffy fur over retractable claws. On four padded paws, he swaggered from the room and through the palace.

At the towering doors of the golden hall, King Kazar, now a homely cat, darted between the shuffling feet of his subjects. He strutted proudly down the carpet to the dais where his brother waited, regally dressed and on a raised platform surrounded by his shadow guards.

At the foot of the throne, when guests were beginning to notice the bold cat, King Kazar shapeshifted back into his regal form. Standing tall, he adjusted his jewel-encrusted turban. Holding his arms wide, he turned to address the crowd.

"Welcome travelers and neighboring kingdoms. For many years, the discordance between the Kingdom of Shapeshifters and the Kingdom of Shadow Walkers has grown. Yesterday, we were two empires divided by distrust. But today, my brother has returned. He will sit on the throne our mother once sat upon and eat at the table our grandfather built. We will align our kingdoms, and our empires will be brothers once again."

He beamed at the merchants, viceroys, chamberlains, and courtiers of each kingdom standing together. *This is what my father would have wanted*, he thought to himself. *United, my enemies will be defeated.* Overcome with joy, he leapt up the stairs of the dais and embraced his brother. He didn't notice the forced smile.

A servant came forward. In her arms, she carried a sparkling crown on a cushion of delicate silk. King Kazar pulled his brother forward and said theatrically, "May I present . . . the Crown of Guilledon."

King Zaeg's eyes raked over the magical crown. His gaze burned with thirst.

"I know you are amused, brother," said King Kazar. "The feast is succulent, the music is spirited. But this crown is enchanted. It will show you the power of shapeshifters. With it, you can see the world as I do. You can roam the earth as any creature you desire. You—"

King Zaeg grabbed for the crown before he finished. The moment his fingers grazed the buffed gold, the crown changed. The metal melted and molded and intertwined around itself. A black turban, pitch as the darkest shadow, with sparkling peridots and blue sapphires took shape.

The crowd gasped and then broke into applause.

King Zaeg placed the turban on his head. The silk rewrapped itself magically.

"You don't seem surprised?" wondered King Kazar.

"No."

"Why? Why are you not . . . ?" his voice trailed off, stunned by the anger on his brother's face.

King Zaeg signaled to his guards, secretly placed around the golden hall. They marched forward, swords clanging, and seized Firoza, the palace guards, the nobles, and then his brother, the king. Firoza and the soldiers drew their weapons, but as they were caught off guard, they were outmatched.

"Yield." King Zaeg demanded.

King Kazar's eyes widened, and his face filled with hurt. "Brother?

"Yield!" King Zaeg shook with anger.

King Kazar nodded. His soldiers dropped their swords, and they were swiftly disarmed.

King Zaeg turned to the startled room. "I am king now. My brother cedes the throne. You are all subject to my rule. From this day, shapeshifting is forbidden."

The crowd looked on fearfully.

"Brother," King Kazar stepped forward, arms raised, but a soldier stopped him with a blade to his chest. "I thought we agreed on peace?"

"Don't speak to me of peace!" King Zaeg spat. "I know of your peace. You think I'm not clever enough to uncover your schemes!"

"What schemes do you speak of?"

"You assembled an army!"

"I am a king," he explained simply.

"They are readied for war!"

King Kazar fumbled as he tried to understand what had led to his brother's betrayal. Why would assembling his army cause his brother distress? "The trolls have pushed into shapeshifter lands and attacked my cities."

A brief flash of surprise flitted across King Zaeg's face. "I have heard nothing of a troll invasion."

"I feared to tell you. We have been at odds for many years, and I needed your support."

He shook off his brother's words. "You promised my lands to the wizards!"

"I did," King Kazar admitted slowly. "Through a treaty. You have pushed your boundaries too far. I had hoped to reason with you. It is rightfully theirs."

"You've expanded your kingdom too," his brother accused in reply.

"I don't deny it. But not the lands of the magic makers. We need the wizards. I'll give you the eastern borders of my lands to account for it."

"You say this now, only because I have your kingdom."

"It was my intention all along. I wish to reunite with my brother and face the trolls together."

"And yet you sent my army to be slaughtered by Jann."

"It was not I but Harun, who lost his life too."

"Dead now, so he cannot refute the blame."

King Kazar flashed angrily. "Be careful of whom you accuse and in whose kingdom you do it!"

"I saw Harun whisper in your ear before he sent them to their death."

"To ask if my soldiers could attack Madrid, the stronger of the jinn. Perhaps had your soldiers been shapeshifters they would have survived."

King Zaeg clenched his fists at his sides, and his face burned red. The promise his brother made to Azhir for the isles sounded in his ears. The field of his dead soldiers burned in his memories. A tiny fleck of dirt from burying his friends wedged in his nails. Even after bathing, he had not been able to wash it all away. For while his brother watched from the sides, he had joined the soldiers and dug the graves. "LIES."

"It is no lie, brother. You see blindly. You judge with partial truths, and truth that is not whole is not truth at all. Calm down and look again. I've assembled this celebration for you. I've had a borlaug's treasure crafted to honor you and welcome you home."

"Welcome me home?" King Zaeg snorted derisively. "You wanted to keep the crown for yourself. I heard you!"

"You spied on me?" King Kazar's voice shook. His patience was slipping away, and he was beginning to match his brother's rage. His subjects looked away, ashamed and afraid.

"Your trickery and dishonesty left me no choice," King Zaeg flared. "Now your kingdom is mine."

"You cannot take the Kingdom of Shapeshifters. They will never follow the rules of the Shadow Kingdom, nor will they take you as their king. Surely you know this."

"I believe I just did."

King Kazar's gaze swept over the banquet and around the golden hall. *Where is Azhir?*

One of his palace soldiers escaped the shadow walker guard, distracting him from his search. The soldier pulled a dagger from his boot and plunged the blade at King Zaeg.

King Kazar reached out. *No!* he breathed, but in his fear, the sound didn't come.

King Zaeg veered to the side, and the tip of the blade scraped down his neck to his shoulder splattering blood on the stone floor.

Blinded by rage, King Zaeg used the crown and shapeshifted. A beast ripped from his chest, and he morphed into a manticore with a lion's body, a scorpion's tail, and enormous dragon wings. He knocked the soldier to the ground, and a metal chain with cuffs clattered on the floor. The manticore roared savagely. Screams pierced the room, and King Kazar's subjects fled. They trampled over one another, pushing for the doors.

King Kazar didn't run. He squared himself defiantly and faced the beast. Brown eyes were all that was left of his brother, but that was enough. "Change back, and we'll speak openly. I will tell you everything."

LOUP GAJIGIANIS

His jaw tightened, and he stood his ground, refusing to show fear. *I need to tread carefully. He doesn't understand the laws of shapeshifters. If he isn't careful, the creature will take control of his instincts, and he will become more beast than magik.*

The manticore spoke in an inhuman growl, "Was I to be taken in chains? Would I have lived in a prison, or would you have sent me to die as you did my soldiers?"

King Kazar took another step, freeing himself from the wall he was cornered in. Firoza grabbed his arm to stop him, but he shrugged free. "It will be okay," he muttered, and with his hands raised in surrender, the shadow guard let him pass. "That would never have happened," he promised his brother.

"More lies!" The manticore lashed its venomous tail and hit a statue. It crumbled and fell in chunks, smashing as it hit the floor. "Concede, or I will take your life as you did my friends."

Firoza moved quickly and caught the shadow soldier off guard. She struck a tender spot beneath his arm, his grip on the sword loosened, and she disarmed him. Another guard closed in to help, and they grappled for control of the weapon.

The Manticore lashed out furiously. His tail hooked around another statue and brought it down over his brother's head.

From a dark corner, where a secret passage was known only to the king, Azhir swept into the hall. His lips moved quickly, and he struck his staff against the stone floor. It came to life, and a deep wave of blue magic rippled from the stone and whipped against the falling statue. The statue cracked, split in two, and the chunks fell on both sides of King Kazar, leaving him unharmed.

Finally, thought King Kazar. Hope swelled in his chest. He didn't want to hurt his brother, and seeing how far his brother's power had come, he didn't believe he could beat him either. With the added magic of the crown, his brother was exceptionally dangerous and unstable. Though he didn't delude himself into thinking the warlock cared for him, at least Azhir didn't abandon him to face his brother alone. Azhir cared for the balance of power and wanted the lands of the wizards returned. That, at least, was enough to tie their fates together and give him a chance at ending this peacefully.

"Stay out of this warlock!" King Zaeg growled.

Azhir uttered softly. His voice echoed off the walls, magnified with magic, and repeated itself a dozen times. "Speak the words!"

King Kazar's head snapped to the warlock. Only he knew what Azhir meant, and their eyes locked. He stuttered—the words stuck inside his throat. He never wanted the curse—not in his heart. He wanted his brother. If only he could make his brother understand.

The manticore growled. Spiked with anger, and unused to the cravings of a wild beast, King Zaeg began to lose control. The beast's grumble turned to a rumbling roar. The last of King Zaeg's brown eyes transfigured, and golden slits glared down at King Kazar. The manticore attacked.

King Kazar stumbled back, shielding his face with his arm.

Clang. Firoza caught the manticore's teeth around her armored cuff. Snarling, the beast bit harder. The armguard snapped, and fangs tore into her flesh. Her eyes widened in pain, and she yanked against the jaw clamping down on her.

"No!" King Kazar sputtered. He blinked, unable to believe what was unfolding before him.

"Get back," Firoza cried out to King Kazar. She was suffering, inches from death, and still trying to protect him.

She swept the hind legs of the lion and used its wings to shield her body from the stinger. Leaning into the lion's clamp on her arm, she tumbled the manticore on its back in one swift move. The beast released her, and blood poured from her veins.

Free of the beast, Firoza drew her sword—

"NO!" King Kazar bellowed. He did not wish to see his brother hurt. *There must be a way to end this peacefully.*

Firoza stopped—her stolen blade inches from the soft fur of the manticore. The beast whirled, its tail flashed, and its stinger sunk deep into Firoza's chest. Her eyes rounded, and she fell back into the arms of her king.

A blood-curdling cry tore from King Kazar's throat. "NO!"

The manticore slunk back. Realizing what he'd done, a soft whine purred shamefully.

Brown eyes teared, the beast faded, and King Zaeg knelt beside Firoza and his brother.

"Why isn't she healing?"

"She's a fairy. Not a changer," King Kazar snapped. "Bring the healer!"

King Zaeg signaled, and the shadow walkers lowered their swords. The guards retrieved their weapons. A few hurried from the golden hall, while others stationed themselves around the room—restoring the order of their king.

King Kazar pulled Firoza upright in his arms and cradled her as she struggled with each breath. His eyes misted, and he pleaded with the warlock. "Azhir! Save her with your magic!"

"I cannot." His tone was stoic.

Offended, King Kazar's head snapped up to glare at Azhir for showing no feelings in his worst moment. But the warlock's face was tormented, and it was clear the warlock endured pain with restraint. "If you're truly the greatest warlock," King Kazar challenged, "then I command you to save her!"

Azhir's eyes bored back into King Kazar's, and he said blankly, "The manticore's stinger is full of poison, and Firoza is a fairy. Magic flows through her whole body. That power is beyond me."

Firoza tried to speak, but the words choked in her chest.

"Shush. You will be fine." Tears spilled down King Kazar's cheeks.

Over the years, Firoza's presence had become part of his daily life. She was like the air in a room and the light on a dark night. She was the energy that livened the palace on the dreariest days as king. She always made sure he was safe. There were many times he had been harsh, and he had not always shown he cared like he should have. As king, he could not show too much favor to one palace sentinel over another. But Firoza was family. She was as close as any brother.

The strength left Firoza. Her eyes fluttered, and her hand drooped. He caught it and held it to his cheek. "Hang on. Help is coming."

"By her own kind, she can be saved. That is the only way. Her blood runs with magic. She needs the care of her own kind."

"If she returns to the Kingdom of Fairies, I'll never see her again! I'm not ready to part from her."

"She cannot be saved here. You must say goodbye. If she doesn't go, she'll die."

King Kazar choked on a sob. He pulled her tighter to her chest and then let her go. "Take her then." He laid Firoza against the stone and whispered in her ear. "Thank you, my friend."

The warlock crouched and lightly touched her shoulder. "I will return shortly." A blue swirl of clouds banged against the windows. It burst through. Shattered pieces of colored glass sprayed across the hall, and the blue cloud swirled around them. Azhir and Firoza disappeared in the spiral of magic, and then they were gone. The glass clattered to the floor, and the hall was silent.

King Kazar stood and faced his brother. His composure fell apart. "I brought you here for peace. Only peace!" He yelled fiercely. "A legion of trolls gather at my border. They mean to kill us all! If they take my kingdom, they'll come for yours next!" His throat ached from shouting. He paced, catching his breath, and then said softer, "I only wished for our kingdoms to align! And face the darker days ahead. After years apart, I was afraid you would not join us! It was that fear that stopped me from telling you sooner."

King Zaeg's eyes dawned. Sorrow swelled in his chest. "I've been a fool. I saw only treachery and deceit. I thought you meant to betray me."

King Kazar raised his chin slightly. Azhir had been right, and he needed to think of his kingdom, and all the lives at stake. "I need to defeat the trolls, and I cannot trust you."

"I am truly sorry for your captain. I didn't know her long, but I respected her."

"Your regret changes nothing. Some choices cannot be undone, no matter how much you wish them." King Kazar pointed to the turban, still resting on his brother's head. The stones glistened black against the candlelight. And he spoke the words.

> "Cast of magic, blood, and stone
> Born the Crown of Guilledon
> Cursed in love, fear, and hate,
> Twisted the metal of our fate
> A veil of good deceives thy nature
> And on my blood, I release thee."

The turban illuminated. An incandescence flushed warmly against the black silk. It spread through King Zaeg, igniting him in a smoldering afterglow. When he was fully ablaze, the glimmer dissipated, leaving a dark coolness.

Bewildered, King Zaeg touched the jeweled turban uncertainly. He blinked and looked around the golden hall, now in crumbles. "What happened?" He locked eyes with his brother and reached out to him, concern and love etched across his face. "Why are you angry? Is everything alright?"

King Kazar softened, feeling the innocence of his younger brother many years past. A thick tear fell down his cheek, but then his eyes settled on the disturbed dust where Firoza had been. Even now, she may be dead. He had been helpless in saving her, though she had protected him for years. And if by some miracle she was alive, the fairy king would never let her return. He wanted her skills for his own kingdom and now he had her. One way or another, she was lost to him forever. His heart chilled. "Take him," King Kazar commanded.

The remaining guards stumbled forward awkwardly, uncertain of the king's command to arrest his brother. The palace soldiers drew their retrieved weapons on the shadow walkers. Metal armor clambered, and they seized King Zaeg. and bound him.

"What's going on?" King Zaeg tried to shadowshift, but nothing happened. "Why can I not transform?"

"Take him to the east tower." King Kazar's jaw hardened. "When our kingdoms are aligned, and all changers live together in harmony—when I've forgiven what happened here today—I will release him from the curse."

The soldiers dragged King Zaeg from the hall, and King Kazar looked away, sickened with hurt and grief. "Leave me!" he commanded, and the room cleared.

When the golden hall was quiet, he knelt where Firoza had fallen—now empty, cold stone. He could almost feel her presence. He remembered the very day it was discovered that she had brought peace to the kingdoms. He was strolling through the Royal Fairy Castle. She was fierce the moment he saw her dragged before the king, though she faced treason. Treason for saving them all.

A majestic figure glided in on a stormy blue cloud and interrupted King Kazar's misery. He looked up at Azhir as he landed on the stone a few feet away. "Don't give me that look, Warlock. Just tell me she lives."

"Firoza will heal. In time."

King Kazar scoured the warlock's face, needing to hear it again. "She lives?"

"She does."

"She lives." A sob escaped, and he almost smiled. He dropped his face in his hands and rubbed his eyes roughly. "But she is gone forever."

Azhir's robes dragged against the stone as he approached. He laid a hand on the king's shoulder. "It's possible for you to care deeply for someone and not have them with you."

"I don't know how."

"With patience. And love for your own life. You must wish her well, and then let her go."

"You ask too much. I have lost my captain and my brother—for when the curse is lifted, he will never forgive me. I want to mope and wallow in peace."

"You now rule both kingdoms," Azhir spoke plainly. "You have pressing concerns that need your attention now. It will be a tremendous weight to bear, as will be uniting the kingdoms, but you must do it all the same."

The king rubbed the wetness from his cheeks and staggered to his feet. Azhir searched his swollen face. "Will you be a good king?"

King Kazar's square jaw flexed, hardening himself for what lay ahead. He met the warlock's gaze and held it. "Until the day comes that the kingdoms rule themselves."

"That sounds like a good beginning."

"I owe it to my brother's—to my kingdom," he corrected, "there must only be one."

"And what of the lands of the wizards?" Azhir quirked a brow.

"Are henceforth returned."

"I shall take my leave then. I suddenly have many things to accomplish. My friends will want to know the good news. And perhaps I can catch a jinni on the way." His eyes twinkled delightfully. "Farewell King Kazar." He murmured a spell, and his staff turned crystal blue. Speckles of light glittered. The robes spun with him. And he vanished.

About the Author

Janet Loup Maupin Gajigianis

Since childhood, Loup wanted to be many things — a jockey, a sailor, a fencer, a treasure hunter, an artist, and even an amateur mixed martial artist. While she wrote short stories as a child, she never imagined she would be an author. Her first book, Magiks and The Crown of Guilledon is available for sale. Book two, Magiks and The Gremlin Thief, is coming soon. Like all things she does, the Enchanted Chronicle series came from the heart. Check out her website at **www.enchantedchronicle.com** where you can get

MAGIKS AND THE TALE OF TWO KINGS

swag, news, updates, upcoming releases, and more details on the incredible world of magiks.

Afterword

While I always had a backstory of the Crown of Guilledon in mind, I sat down to write it when a friend and fellow author asked me to submit a story for an exciting anthology he was creating. If my story was good enough it would be included with approximately ten other stories by various authors—and well, of course I hoped that it would be.

At this time in my life, I was facing an 'unexpected situation' that profoundly steered the messages I wanted to convey in the subtext of this fantastical story. One that told of mythical creatures, war, and the creation of the Crown of Guilledon.

Someone close to me, with little time invested to know me, judged me falsely. He went online and both mocked and ridiculed observances he construed in his mind to be my own thoughts and characteristics. What he doesn't know, is that I saw the whole live stream.

So came the story of the Two Kings who fell for the Fallacy of Perception.

I believe that it's debatable whether or not there is a clear declaration of the Fallacy of Perception, but for me, and every one of you reading this, it exists.

For those of you who don't know of human fallacies, there is not, I believe, a definitive number. But the meaning is clear. A fallacy is an error a human makes in his or her reasoning that leads to an error in judgement or in action. These errors emerge from mistakes in reasoning, logic, understanding of observations, misinterpretation of arguments, and mistakes in deductive or inductive reasoning, etc.

So now to the story. . . .

King Kazar and King Zaeg (characters that I had created years prior) form opinions and perspectives based off limited information and erred judgement, and it leads to losses on both sides. While King Zaeg loses his kingdom, King Kazar loses a dear friend and ally.

I hope the message in this story teaches all of us to take a little more time before judging someone. People only put forth the information that they want others to know, and there is a whole lot more to everyone that any one of us can decipher in superficial, daily conversation.

Now that we have delved deeper into the underlying message, let's talk about some more hidden context.

Each chapter highlights one of the characters and a stimulus, which based on the character's choices, did or did not affect the story.

The Return of the Prince: Named after the way King Kazar sees his lost brother. Zaeg left as a prince and became a mighty king. The stimulus is the younger brother's (Zaeg's) return to his father's kingdom as the bequest of his older brother (Kazar). This is the beginning of the short story.

The Warrior's Wisdom: Chosen from the warning Firoza gave to King Zaeg. If her advice had been heeded, it might have ended the entire plot. Based on Zaeg's choice, her advice did not impact the story.

The Warlock's Guile: Perhaps my favorite chapter was perfectly named after the deceptive choice Azhir made that altered the history of changers and years later, led to the war between shapeshifters and shadow walkers. Guile means deceit by intention and usually through wit. Guile played a role in the creation of the word Guilledon. I added an extra "l" because I thought it looked better. I chose the suffix don because of the meaning 'to put on'. It is pronounced Guile-don with a soft roll from the i to the l.

The Jinn's Way: The highlighted characters in this title are the two jinn. Way can be interpreted as the jinn's mannerisms, their desires, or as a synonym used in place of path. Like the metaphorical path that was unrivaled when Jann slaughtered the shadow king's army who attacked at the direction of General Harun of the shapeshifter army. That riled the growing distance between the two brothers.

The Shadow's Choice: King Zaeg spends a lot of time in his shadow form. I wanted to highlight the sly shadow separately from his charismatic human form, almost like a second character. In the fleeting moment where Madrid is about to kill King Kazar, the shadow chooses to save him. He kills the jinni and saves his brother despite his belief that Kazar intended to betray him and despite his belief that his army was set up by his brother. In that fleeting moment, the shadow could have let the jinni kill his brother—he could have killed his brother himself—or he could save his brother. He saved his brother. But why? Do we assume he had a good heart? Was there still love for his brother? Was it an accident, and the jinni stepped in front of his attack? We don't know exactly because the viewpoint of the chapter belonged to the warlock. We can only know what the warlock believes or observes.

The King's Fallacy: Named after the king's Fallacy of Perception that led to Firoza's near death, return to the land of fairies, and ultimately the war between changers. But which king had the greater fallacy? Was it the younger brother that acted in his misinterpretation of the things he observed? Or was it the older brother who misjudged his younger brother's thoughts and interpretations and withheld vital information that would have steered the story into a whole new plot? That is for you to decide.

Made in United States
North Haven, CT
05 September 2024